"My sons think I've gone and lost my marbles,"

Harlan said, chuckling.

Startled, Janet simply stared at him. "Why would they think a thing like that?"

Harlan's gaze drifted over her slowly and with unmistakable intent. "Because I'm just crazy enough to think about courting a woman like you."

Janet swallowed hard at the blunt response. "Harlan, I don't want you to get the wrong idea here."

He reached over and patted her hand consolingly, then winked. "Darlin', there is absolutely nothing wrong with the ideas I have. You'll have to trust me on that."

That, of course, was the problem. She didn't trust him, or, for that matter, herself. She had a feeling a man with Harlan's confidence and determination could derail her plans for her life in the blink of an eye.

And she wasn't sure if she was scared...or excited.

Dear Reader,

Welcome to Silhouette **Special Edition**...welcome to romance. March has six wonderful books in store for you that are guaranteed to become some of your all-time favorites!

Our THAT SPECIAL WOMAN! title for March is *Sisters* by Penny Richards. A dramatic and emotional love story, this book about family and the special relationship between a mother and daughter is one you won't want to miss!

Also in March, it's time to meet another of the irresistible Adams men in the new series by Sherryl Woods, AND BABY MAKES THREE, which continues with *The Rancher and His Unexpected Daughter*. And continuing this month is Pamela Toth's newest miniseries, BUCKLES AND BRONCOS. In *Buchanan's Baby*, a cowboy is hearing wedding bells and the call of fatherhood. Rounding out the month are *For Love of Her Child*, a touching and emotional story from Tracy Sinclair, Diana Whitney's *The Reformer*, the next tale in her THE BLACKTHORN BROTHERHOOD series, and *Playing Daddy* by Lorraine Carroll.

These books are sure to make the month of March an exciting and unforgettable one! I hope you enjoy these books, and all the stories to come!

Sincerely,

Tara Gavin
Senior Editor

Please address questions and book requests to:
Silhouette Reader Service
U.S.: 3010 Walden Ave., P.O. Box 1325, Buffalo, NY 14269
Canadian: P.O. Box 609, Fort Erie, Ont. L2A 5X3

Sherryl Woods

THE RANCHER AND HIS UNEXPECTED DAUGHTER

Published by Silhouette Books

America's Publisher of Contemporary Romance

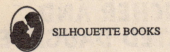

SILHOUETTE BOOKS

ISBN 0-373-24016-3

THE RANCHER AND HIS UNEXPECTED DAUGHTER

SHERRYL WOODS

lives by the ocean, which, she says, provides daily inspiration for the romance in her soul. She further explains that her years as a television critic taught her about steamy plots and humor; her years as a travel editor took her to exotic locations; and her years as a crummy weekend tennis player taught her to stick with what she enjoyed most—writing. "What better way is there," Sherryl asks, "to combine all that experience than by creating romantic stories?" Sherryl loves to hear from her readers. You may write to her at P.O. Box 490326, Key Biscayne, FL 33149. A self-addressed stamped envelope is appreciated for a reply.

It's legal and binding!
Harlan Adams and
Janet Runningbear
are the proud parents
of two daughters:
Jenny Runningbear Adams
and
their latest acquisition
Mary Elizabeth Adams,
born March 4 at 2:12 p.m.

Chapter One

Harlan Adams walked out of Rosa's Mexican Café after eating his fill of her spicy brand of Tex-Mex food just in time to see his pickup barrel down the center of Main Street at fifty miles an hour. In the sleepy Texas town of Los Piños, both the theft and the speed were uncommon occurrences.

"Ain't that your truck?" Mule Masters asked, staring after the vehicle that was zigzagging all over the road, endangering parked cars and pedestrians alike.

"Sure as hell is," Harlan said, indignation making his insides churn worse than Rosa's hot sauce.

"That's what you get for leaving your keys in plain sight. I've been telling you for months now that times have changed. The world's full of thieves and murderers,'' Mule said ominously. ''They were bound to get to Los Piños sooner or later.''

Given the time it was wasting, Harlan found the familiar lecture extremely irritating. ''Where's your car?'' he snapped.

Mule blinked at the sharp tone. ''Across the street, right where it always is.''

Harlan was already striding across the two-lane road before the words were completely out of his friend's mouth. ''Come on, old man.''

Mule appeared vaguely startled by the command. ''Come on where?''

''To catch the damned thing, that's where,'' he replied with a certain amount of eagerness. The thought of a good ruckus held an amazing appeal.

''Sheriff's close by,'' Mule objected without picking up speed.

Harlan lost patience with the procrastinating that had earned Mule his nickname. ''Just give me your keys,'' he instructed. He didn't take any chances on Mule's compliance. He reached out and snatched them from his friend's hand.

Before the old man could even start grumbling, Harlan was across the street and starting the engine of a battered old sedan. That car had seen a hundred thousand hard miles or more back and forth across the state of Texas, thanks to Mule's knack for tinkering with an engine.

Harlan pulled out onto Main Street, gunned the engine a couple of times, then shifted gears with pure pleasure. The smooth glide from standing stock-still to sixty in the blink of an eye was enough to make a man weep.

In less than a minute his truck was in sight again on the outskirts of town and he was gaining on it. He was tempted to whoop with joy at the sheer exhilaration of the impromptu race, but he had to keep every bit of his energy focused on his pursuit of that runaway truck.

The chase lasted just long enough to stir his ire, but not nearly long enough to be downright interesting. Not a mile out of town, where the two-lane road curved like a well-rounded lady's hips, he caught up with the truck just in time to see it miss the turn and swerve straight toward a big, old, cottonwood tree. His heart climbed straight into his throat and stayed there as he watched the drama unfold.

He veered from the highway onto the shoulder and slammed on his own brakes just as the truck collided with the tree. It hit with a resounding *thwack* that crumpled the front fender on the passenger side, sent his blood pressure soaring, and elicited a string of profanity from inside the truck that blistered his ears.

''What the devil?'' he muttered as he scrambled from the borrowed car and ran toward the truck. Obviously the thief couldn't be badly injured if he had that much energy left for cursing.

To his astonishment, when he flung open the driver's door, a slender young girl practically tumbled out into his arms. He righted her, keeping a firm clamp on her wrist in case the little thief decided to flee.

She couldn't be a day over thirteen, he decided, gazing into scared brown eyes. Admittedly, though, she had a vocabulary that a much older dock worker would envy. She also had a belligerent tilt to her cute little chin and a sullen expression that dared him to yell at her.

Taken aback by her apparent age, Harlan bit back the shouted lecture he'd planned and settled for a less confrontative approach. He could hardly wait to hear why this child had stolen his pickup.

"You okay?" he inquired quietly. Other than a bump on her forehead, he couldn't see any other signs of injury.

She wriggled in a game effort to free herself from his grip. He grinned at the wasted attempt. He'd wrestled cows ten times her weight or more. This little slip of a thing didn't stand a chance of getting away until he was good and ready to let her go. He didn't plan on that happening anytime soon. Not until he had the answers he wanted, anyway.

"Must be just fine, if you can struggle like that," he concluded out loud. "Any particular reason you decided to steal my truck?"

"I was tired of walking," she shot back.

"Did you ever consider a bike?"

"Not fast enough," she muttered, her gaze defiantly clashing with his.

"You had someplace to get to in a hurry?"

She shrugged.

Harlan had to fight to hide a grin. He'd always been a big admirer of audacity, though he preferred it to be a little better directed. "What's your name?"

She frowned and for the first time began to look faintly uneasy. "Who wants to know?"

"I'm Harlan Adams. I own White Pines. That's a ranch just outside of town." If she was local, that would be plenty of explanation to intimidate her. If she wasn't, he could elaborate until he had her quivering with fear in her dusty sneakers for pulling a stunt like the one that had ended with his pickup wrapped around a tree.

"Big deal," she retorted, then let loose a string of expletives.

She either wasn't local or it was going to take a lot more to impress her with the stupidity of what she'd done. "You have a foul mouth, you know that?" he observed.

"So?"

"I'll just bet you don't talk that way around your mama."

The mention of her mother stirred an expression of pure alarm on her delicate features. Harlan sensed that he'd hit the nail on the head. This ragamuffin kid with the sleek black hair cut as short as a boy's, with the high cheekbones and tanned complexion, might not be afraid of him, but she was scared to death of her mother. He considered it a hopeful sign. He was very big on respect for parental authority, not that he'd noticed his grown-up sons paying the concept much mind lately.

"You're not going to tell her, are you?" she asked, clearly trying to keep the worry out of her voice and failing miserably. For the first time since she'd climbed out of his truck, she sounded her age.

"Now why would I want to keep quiet about the fact that you stole my truck and slammed it into a tree?"

A resurgence of belligerence glinted in her eyes. "Because she'll sue you for pain and suffering. I'm almost positive I've got a whiplash injury," she said, rubbing at her neck convincingly. "Probably back problems that'll last the rest of my life, too."

Harlan chuckled. "Imagine that. All those problems and you expect to blame them on the man whose truck you stole and smashed up. You and your mother have a little scam going? You wreck cars and she sues for damages?"

At the criticism of her mother's ethics, her defiance wavered just a little. "My mom's a lawyer," she admitted eventually. "She sues lots of people." Her eyes glittered with triumphant sparks as she added, "She wins, too."

An image suddenly came to him, an image of the new lawyer he'd read about just last week in the local paper. The article had been accompanied by a picture of an incredibly lovely woman, her long black hair flowing down her back, her features and her name strongly suggesting her Comanche heritage. Janet Something-or-other. Runningbear, maybe. Yep, that was it. Janet Runningbear.

He surveyed the girl standing in front of him and thought he detected a resemblance. There was no mistaking the Native American genes in her proud bearing, her features or her coloring, though he had a hunch they'd been mellowed by a couple of generations of interracial marriage.

"Your mom's the new lawyer in town, then," he said. "Janet Runningbear."

She seemed startled that he'd guessed, but she hid it quickly behind another of those belligerent looks she'd obviously worked hard to perfect. "So?"

"So, I think you and I need to go have a little chat with your mama," he said, putting a hand on the middle of her back and giving her a gentle but unrelenting little push in the direction of Mule's car. Her chin rose another notch, but her shoulders slumped and she didn't resist. In fact, there was an air of weary resignation about her that tugged at his heart.

As he drove back into town he couldn't help wondering just how much trouble Janet Runningbear's daughter managed to get herself into on a regular basis and why she felt the need to do it. After raising four sons of his own, he knew a whole lot about teenage rebellion and the testing of parental authority. He'd always thought—mistakenly apparently— that girls might have been easier. Not that he would have traded a single one of his boys to find out firsthand. He'd planned on keeping an eye on his female grandbabies to test his theory.

He glanced over at the slight figure next to him and caught the downward turn of her mouth and the protective clasping of her arms across her chest. Stubbornness radiated from every pore. The prospect of meeting the woman who had raised such a little hellion intrigued him.

It was the first time since a riding accident had taken his beloved Mary away from him the year before that he'd found much of anything fascinating.

He realized as the blood zinged through his veins for the first time in months just how boring and predictable he'd allowed his life to become.

He'd left the running of the ranch mostly in Cody's hands, just as his youngest son had been itching for him to do for some time. Harlan spent his days riding over his land or stopping off in town to have lunch and play a few hands of poker with Mule or some other friend. His evenings dragged out endlessly unless one or the other of his sons stopped by for a visit and brought his grandbabies along.

For a rancher who'd crammed each day to its limits all his life, he'd been telling himself that the tedium was a welcome relief. He'd been convinced of it, too, until the instant when he'd seen his truck barreling down Main Street.

Something about the quick, hot surge of blood in his veins told him those soothing, dull days were over. Glancing down at the ruffian by his side, he could already anticipate the upcoming encounter with any woman bold and brash enough to keep her in hand. He suddenly sensed that he was just about to start living again.

Janet Runningbear gazed out of the window of her small law office on Main Street and saw her daughter being ushered down the sidewalk by a man she recognized at once as Harlan Adams, owner of White Pines and one of the most successful ranchers for several hundred miles in any direction. Judging from the stern expression on his face and Jenny's dragging footsteps, her daughter had once more gotten herself into a mess of trouble.

She studied the man approaching with a mixture of trepidation, anger, and an odd, tingly hint of anticipation. Ever since her move to Los Piños, the closest town to where her ancestors had once lived, she'd been hearing about Harlan Adams, the man whose own ancestors had been at least in part responsible for pushing the Comanches out of Texas and onto an Oklahoma reservation.

The claiming of Comanche lands might have taken place a hundred years or more ago, but Janet clung to the resentment that had been passed down to her by her great-grandfather. Lone Wolf had lived to be ninety-seven and his father had been forced from the nomadic life of a hunter to the confined space of a reservation.

Even though she knew it was ridiculous to blame Harlan Adams for deeds that had been committed long before his birth or her own, she was prepared to dislike him just on principle. What she hadn't been prepared for was the prompt and very feminine response to a man who practically oozed sex appeal from every masculine pore.

He was cowboy through and through, from the Stetson hat that rode atop his thick, sun-streaked hair to the tips of his dusty boots. His weathered face hinted at his age, which she knew to be somewhere in his fifties, but nothing about his easy stride or his broad shoulders added to that impression. He had the bearing of a much younger man.

In fact, Harlan Adams strolled down the sidewalk, her daughter in tow, with the confidence of a man who was comfortable with himself and with the power his wealth had earned him. To dampen any spark of fascination he might arouse, Janet quickly assured herself it was more than confidence she saw. It was arrogance, a trait she despised. Since there was no mistaking his destination, she braced herself for his arrival.

A few minutes later, with the pair of them seated across from her, she listened with a sense of growing horror as Harlan Adams described the theft of his truck and the subsequent accident, which had clearly done more damage to the truck than it had to Jenny. Her daughter didn't even seem flustered.

"He shouldn't have left the damned keys inside," Jenny muttered.

"Watch your tongue, young lady," Janet warned.

A heartfelt apology rose to Janet's lips but before she could begin to form the words, she caught a surprising glint of amusement in Harlan's startlingly blue eyes. She'd been anticipating the same mischievous dark brown eyes each of his sons reportedly had, according to the fond reminiscences of the local ladies. They must have inherited those from their mother, she decided. Harlan's were the bright blue of a summer sky just rinsed by rain.

"Jenny, perhaps you should wait in the other room, while Mr. Adams and I discuss this," she said, sensing that the twinkle in those eyes might mean an inclination toward leniency that wasn't altogether deserved.

The last of her daughter's defiance slid away. "Am I going to jail?" she asked in a voice that shook even though she was clearly trying desperately to sound brave.

"That remains to be seen," Janet told her without so much as a hint that she thought jail was the last thing on this particular victim's mind.

"Are you going to be my lawyer?"

Janet hid her face so that Jenny wouldn't see her own smile. "If you need one," she promised solemnly, doubting that it was going to come to that.

Sure enough, the second Jenny was out of the room, Harlan Adams chuckled. "Damn, but she's a pistol. She's got the makings of one heck of a young woman."

"If she doesn't self-destruct first," Janet muttered wearily. "I'm not sure I understand why you find all of this so amusing."

He grinned at her and her heart did an unexpected little flip. There was something so unexpectedly boyish about that lazy, lopsided smile. At the same time, the experience and wisdom that shone in his eyes was comforting. Something told her at once that this was a man a woman could always count on for straight talk and moral support. A little of that misguided resentment she'd been stoking slipped away.

"Remind me to tell you about the time one of my boys rustled a bunch of my cattle to start his own herd," Harlan Adams said, still chuckling over the memory. "He was seven at the time. Try taking your daughter's mischief and multiply it four times over and you'll have some idea why I can't work up too much of a sweat over one stolen truck.''

"She could have been killed," Janet said grimly, realizing as she spoke that she was shaking at the very thought of what could have happened to Jenny.

"But she wasn't," Harlan reminded her in a soothing tone that suggested he knew exactly the sort of belated reaction she was having.

"Then there's the matter of your truck. I'm just getting my practice off the ground here, but I can make arrangements to pay you back over time, if that's okay.''

He waved off the offer. "Insurance will take care of it."

"But it's my responsibility," she insisted.

"The danged truck's not important," he countered emphatically. "The real question now is how to make sure that gal of yours doesn't go trying some fool thing like that again."

His unexpected kindness brought the salty sting of tears to her eyes. Janet rubbed at them impatiently. She never cried. Never. In fact, she considered it a point of honor that she was always strong and in control.

Suddenly, for some reason she couldn't fathom, she was not only crying, but actually considering spilling her guts to a total stranger. Harlan Adams was practically the first person in town to be civilized to her, much less kind. Truth be told, the move to Texas was not turning out anything at all the way she'd imagined it would.

"I'm sorry," she apologized. "I don't know what's wrong with me or with Jenny. I never cry. And she used to be such a good girl."

Harlan's expression remained solemn and thoughtful. "You know," he said, "I used to teach my sons that tears made a man seem weak. The past year or so, I've had a change of heart. I think it takes someone pretty strong to acknowledge when they're feeling vulnerable and then deal straight-out with the pain they're going through."

Janet guessed right off that it was his wife's death that had brought him to a change of heart. The word on Mary Adams was mixed, according to the gossip that folks had been eager to share. Some thought she'd been an elegant, refined lady. Others thought she was a cold, uppity witch. One thing no one disputed, however, was that Harlan Adams had adored her and that she had doted on him.

Janet had wondered more than once what it would be like to love anyone with such passion. Her own marriage had been lukewarm at best and certainly not up to the kind of tests it had been put through. She'd been relieved to call it quits, eager to move far from New York and its memories to the land Lone Wolf had described with such bittersweet poignancy. She had legally taken the name he'd dubbed her with as soon as she'd settled in town. A new name, a fresh start for her and Jenny.

She glanced up and realized that Harlan's warm gaze was fixed on her. He was regarding her with more of that compassion that made her want to weep.

"Why don't you tell me what's been going on with that girl of yours?" he offered. "Maybe we can figure this thing out together."

Surprised at the relief she felt at having someone with whom to share her concerns, Janet tried to describe what the past few weeks had been like. "I thought coming here was going to make such a difference for Jenny," she said. "Instead, she's behaving as if I've punished her by moving from New York to Texas."

"Quite a change for a young girl," Harlan observed. "She's at an age when leaving all her friends behind must seem like the end of the world. Hell, she's at an age when *everything* seems like the end of the world. Besides that, it's summertime. All the kids her age around here are caught up with their own vacation activities. Lots of 'em have to work their family's ranch. Must seem like she'll never have a friend of her own again."

Janet didn't like having a total stranger tell her something she should have figured out for herself. She'd been so anxious to get to Texas after the divorce, so determined to get on with her life and to get Jenny settled in a safer environment than the city streets of Manhattan that she hadn't given much thought to how lonely the summer might be for her daughter. She'd been thinking of the move as an adventure and had assumed Jenny was doing the same.

Now it appeared that the kind of energy that might have resulted in little more than mischief back in New York was taking a dangerous turn. She cringed as she pictured that truck slamming into a tree with her daughter behind the wheel. If her ex-husband heard about that, he'd wash his hands of Jenny once and for all. Barry Randall had little enough room in his life for his daughter now. If she became a liability to his image, he'd forget she existed.

"I have an idea," the man seated across from her said. "I don't intend to press charges for this, but we don't want her getting the idea that she can get away with stealing a car and taking it joyriding."

Janet was so worried by the prospects for Jenny getting herself into serious trouble before school started in the fall that she was willing to listen to anything, even if it was being offered by the exact kind of man she'd learned to distrust—a rich and powerful white man. A Texan, to boot. A sworn enemy of her ancestors.

"What?" she asked warily.

"I'll give her a job out at White Pines. She can earn enough to pay off the cost of the truck's repairs. That'll keep her busy, teach her to take responsibility for her actions, and wear her out at the same time."

"I said I'd pay," Janet reminded him.

"It's not the same. It was her mistake."

Just one of many lately, Janet thought with a sigh. Perhaps if Jenny hadn't shoplifted a whole handful of cosmetics from the drugstore the week before, perhaps if she hadn't upended a table in Rosa's Café breaking every dish on it, Janet might have resisted a suggestion that would have kept her in contact with this man who made her pulse skip. The kindness in his voice, the humor in his eyes, were every bit as dangerous to her in her beleaguered state of mind as Jenny's exploits were to her future. At the rate she'd been going since they got to Texas, she'd either end up in jail or dead.

"Do I have any choice?" she asked, all but resigned to accepting the deal he was offering.

He shrugged. "Not really. I could sue you, I suppose, but that gal of yours says you're the best lawyer around. You might win, and then where would I be?"

Janet laughed at the outrageous comment. A man who could keep his sense of humor in a circumstance like this was rare. She just might be forced to reevaluate Harlan Adams. And he might be just the kind of good influence her daughter needed. There was no question Jenny needed a stern hand and perhaps a stronger father figure than her own daddy had ever provided.

"Are you really sure you want to deal with a rebellious teenage girl for the rest of the summer?" she asked, but there was no denying the hopeful note in her voice as she envisioned an improvement in Jenny's reckless behavior.

"I'll take my chances," he said solemnly, his gaze fixed on her.

Janet trembled at the speculative gleam she saw in his eyes. She hadn't had this kind of immediate, purely sexual reaction to a man in a very long time. She'd actually convinced herself she was capable of controlling such things. Now not only was Jenny out of control, it appeared her hormones were, as well. It was a dismaying turn of events.

It also served as a warning that she'd better be on her guard around Harlan Adams. It wouldn't do to spend much time around him with her defenses down. He was the kind of man who'd claim what he wanted, just as his ancestors had. Whether it was land or a woman probably wouldn't matter much.

She adopted her most businesslike demeanor, the one she reserved for clients and the courtroom. "What time do you want her at White Pines?" she inquired briskly, prepared to temporarily sacrifice her emotional peace of mind for her daughter's sake.

"Dawn will do," he said as he rose and headed for the door.

He must have heard her faint gasp of dismay because he turned back and winked. "I'll have the coffee ready when you get there."

Janet sighed as he walked away. *Dawn!* If he expected her to be coherent at that hour, he'd better have gallons of it and it had best be strong and black.

Chapter Two

"I've taken on another hand for the summer," Harlan mentioned to Cody when he stopped by just before dinner later that night.

His son sat up a little straighter in the leather chair in which he'd sprawled out of habit as soon as he'd walked through the door. Instantly Harlan could see Cody's jaw setting stubbornly as he prepared to argue against his father's unilateral decision. Harlan decided he'd best cut him off at the pass.

"Don't go getting your drawers in a knot," he advised him. "I'm not usurping your authority. This was just something that came up."

"Came up how?" Cody asked, suspicion written all over his face. "There's no budget for another hand. You told me that yourself when we talked about it just last week.''

''It came up right after my truck was stolen and smashed up,'' Harlan explained. ''Let's just say that no money will be changing hands. The thief will be working off the repair bill.''

Cody's jaw dropped. ''You hired the thief who stole your car? Haven't you ever heard of jail time? If any of us had stolen a car and gone joyriding, you'd have helped the sheriff turn the lock on the cell.''

''It didn't seem like the thing to do with a thirteen-year-old girl,'' Harlan said mildly. ''Seemed to me this was a better way to teach her a lesson.''

Cody fell silent, clearly chewing over the concept of a teenage girl as his newest ranch hand. ''What the hell am I supposed to have her doing?'' he asked finally.

''You're not her boss,'' Harlan said, amused by the relief that instantly spread across Cody's face. ''I am. I just wanted you to know she'd be around. Her name's Jenny Runningbear.''

''Runningbear? Is her mother...?''

''The new lawyer in town,'' Harlan supplied, watching as curiosity rose in Cody's eyes.

''Did you meet her?'' Cody asked.

''I did.'' He decided then and there that he'd better be stingy with information about that meeting. His son had the look of a man about to make a romantic mountain out of a platonic molehill.

''And?''

''And, what?''

"What did you think of her?"

"She seemed nice," Harlan offered blandly, even as he conjured up some fairly steamy images of the raven-haired beauty who'd struck him as a fascinating blend of strength and vulnerability. *Nice* was far too tame a description for that delicate, exotic face, those long, long legs, and eyes so dark a man could lose himself in them.

"Really?" Cody said, skepticism written all over his face. "Nice?"

Harlan didn't like the way Cody was studying him. "That's what I said, isn't it?" he replied irritably.

"Just seemed sort of namby-pamby to me," Cody retorted. "I might have described her as hot. I believe Jordan said something similar after he spotted her."

Harlan bit back a sharp rebuke. His gaze narrowed. "Exactly how well do you and your brother know the woman?"

"Not well enough to say more than hello when we pass on the street. Never even been introduced. Of course, if we both weren't happily married, we'd probably be brawling over first dibs on meeting her."

"See that you remember that you are married," he advised his son.

"Interesting," Cody observed, his eyes suddenly sparkling with pure mischief.

"What's interesting?"

"The way you're getting all protective about the mother of a teenage car thief. What time are they getting here in the morning?"

"That's nothing you need to concern yourself about." He stood, glanced at his watch pointedly as he anticipated his housekeeper's imminent announcement that dinner was on the table. "I'd invite you to dinner, but I told Maritza I'd be eating alone. It's time you got home to your wife and those grandbabies of mine anyway."

Cody didn't budge. "They're eating in town with her folks tonight, so I'm all yours. I told Maritza I'd be staying. I thought maybe we could wrangle a little over buying that acreage out to the east, but I'd rather talk more about your impressions of Janet Runningbear."

"Forget it," Harlan warned. "Besides, since when does my housekeeper take orders from you?"

Cody grinned. "Ever since I was old enough to talk. I inherited your charm. It pays off in the most amazing ways. Maritza even fixed all my favorites. She said she'd missed me something fierce. I'm the one with the cast-iron stomach."

Harlan sighed as he thought of the hot peppers that comment implied. Between lunch at Rosa's and that darned accident, his own stomach could have used a bowl of nice bland oatmeal. It appeared he was out of luck.

"Well, come on, then. The sooner we eat, the sooner I can get you out of here and get some peace and quiet."

"You really interested in peace and quiet, Daddy? Or do you just want to make sure you get some beauty sleep before you see Janet Runningbear in the morning?" Cody taunted.

"Don't go getting too big for your britches, son," Harlan warned. "You're not so old that I can't send you packing without your supper. Push me hard enough, I might just send you packing, period."

"But you won't," Cody retorted confidently.

"Oh? Why is that?"

"Because so far only you and I know about this new fascination of yours. Send me home and I'll have the whole, long evening to fill up. I might decide to use that time by calling Luke and Jordan. They like to be up-to-date on everything that goes on around White Pines. They'll be flat-out delighted to discover that you're no longer bored."

Harlan could just imagine the hornet's nest that would stir up. He'd have all three sons hovering over him, making rude remarks, discussing his relationship with a woman he'd barely spent a half hour with up to now. They'd consider taunting him their duty, just as he'd considered it his to meddle in their lives.

"That's blackmail," he accused.

Cody's grin was unrepentant. "Sure is. It's going to make life around here downright interesting, isn't it?"

Harlan sighed. It was indeed.

"I don't see why I have to work for him," Jenny declared for the hundredth time since learning of the agreement her mother had made with Harlan Adams. "Aren't there child labor laws or something?"

"There are also laws against car theft," Janet stated flatly. "You didn't seem overly concerned about those."

A yawn took a little of the edge off of her words. No one in his right mind actually got up at daybreak. She was certain of it. Even though she'd forced herself to get to bed two hours earlier than usual the night before, she'd wanted to hurl the alarm clock out the window when it had gone off forty-five minutes ago.

She'd dressed in a sleepy fog. With any luck, everything at least matched. As for her driving, she would probably be considered a menace if anyone checked on how many of her brain cells were actually functioning. The lure of a huge pot of caffeinated coffee was all that had gotten her out the door.

At the moment she could cheerfully have murdered Jenny for getting them into this predicament. The very thought of doing this day after day all summer long had her gnashing her teeth. She was in no mood for any more of her daughter's backtalk.

"Why couldn't you just pay him?" Jenny muttered. "There's money in my account from Dad."

"It's for college," Janet reminded her. "Besides, I offered to pay Mr. Adams. He refused."

"Jeez, did he see you coming! I'm free labor, Mom. He'll probably have me scrubbing down the barn floor or something. I'll probably end up with arthritis from kneeling in all that cold, filthy water."

"Serves you right," Janet said.

At the lack of either sympathy or any hint of a reprieve, Jenny retreated into sullen silence. That gave Janet time to work on her own composure.

To her astonishment, Harlan Adams had slipped into her dreams last night. She'd awakened feeling restless and edgy and unfulfilled in a way that didn't bear too close a scrutiny. It was a state she figured she'd better get over before her arrival at White Pines. He had struck her as the kind of man who would seize on any hint of weakness and capitalize on it.

The sun was just peeking over the horizon in a blaze of brilliant orange when she arrived at the gate to the ranch. She turned onto the property with something akin to awe spreading through her as she studied the raw beauty of the land around her. This was the land Lone Wolf had described, lush and barren in turns, stretched out as far as the eye could see, uninterrupted by the kind of development she'd come to take for granted in New York.

"This is it?" Jenny asked, a heavy measure of disdain in her voice. "There's nothing here."

Janet hid a smile. No Bloomingdale's. No high rises. No restaurants or music stores. It was little wonder her daughter sounded so appalled.

She, to the contrary, was filled at last with that incredible sense of coming home that she'd wanted so badly to feel when she'd moved to Los Piños. She considered for a moment whether Lone Wolf's father might have hunted on this very land. It pleased her somehow to think that he might have.

"That's why they call it the wide open spaces," she told her daughter. "Remember all the stories I told you about Lone Wolf?"

"Yeah, but I don't get it," Jenny declared flatly. "Maybe I could just get a job in the drugstore or something and pay Mr. Adams back that way."

"No," Janet said softly, listening to the early morning sounds of birds singing, insects humming and somewhere in the distance a tractor rumbling. Did he grow his own grain? Or maybe have a nice vegetable garden? On some level, she thought she'd been waiting all her life for a moment just like this.

"I think this will be perfect for you," she added as hope flowered inside her for the first time in years.

Jenny rolled her eyes. "If he makes me go near a horse or a cow, I'm out of here," she warned.

Janet grinned. "This is a cattle ranch. I think you can pretty much count on horses and cows."

"Mo-om!" she wailed. Her gaze narrowed. "I'll run away. I'll steal a car and drive all the way home to New York."

"And then what?" Janet inquired mildly. Jenny knew as well as she did that there was no room for her in her father's life. Even though at the moment his selfishness suited her purposes, she hated Barry Randall for making his disinterest so abundantly clear to his daughter.

Jenny turned a tearful gaze on her that almost broke Janet's heart.

"I don't have a choice, do I?" she asked.

"Afraid not, love. Besides, I think you'll enjoy this once you've gotten used to it. Think of all the stories you'll have to write to your friends back in New York. How many of them have ever seen a genuine cowboy, much less worked on a ranch?"

"How many of them even wanted to?" Jenny shot back.

"You remember what I always told my clients when they landed in jail?" Janet asked.

Jenny shot her a tolerant look and sighed heavily. "I remember. It's up to me whether I make my time here hard or easy."

"Exactly."

A sudden gleam lit her eyes. "I suppose it's also up to me whether it's hard or easy for Mr. Adams, too, huh?"

Janet didn't much like the sound of that. "Jenny," she warned. "If you don't behave, you'll be in debt to this man until you're old enough for college."

"I'll be good, Mom. Cross my heart."

Janet nodded, accepting the promise, but the glint in her daughter's eyes when she made that solemn vow was worrisome. The words had come a little too quickly, a little too easily. Worse, she recognized that glint all too well. It made her wonder if Harlan Adams just might have bitten off more than he could handle.

One look at him a few minutes later and her doubts vanished. This was a man competent to deal with anything at all. When he rounded the corner of the house in his snug, worn jeans, his blue chambray shirt, his dusty boots and that Stetson hat, he almost stole her breath away.

If she was ever of a mind to let another man into her life, she wanted one who exuded exactly this combination of strength, sex appeal and humor. His eyes were practically dancing with laughter as he approached. And the appreciative head-to-toe look he gave her could have melted steel. Her knees didn't stand a chance. They turned weak as a new colt's.

"Too early for you?" he inquired, his gaze drifting over her once more in the kind of lazy inspection that left goose bumps in its wake.

"No, indeed," she denied brightly. "Why would you think that?"

"No special reason. It's just that you struck me as a woman who'd never leave the house with quite so many buttons undone."

A horrified glance at her blouse confirmed the teasing comment. She'd missed more buttons than she'd secured, which meant there was an inordinate amount of cleavage revealed. She vowed to strangle her daughter at the very first opportunity for not warning her. At least the damned blouse did match her slacks, she thought as she fumbled with the buttons with fingers that shook.

"Jeez, Mom," Jenny protested. "Let me."

Janet thought she heard Harlan mutter something that sounded suspiciously like, "Or me," but she couldn't be absolutely sure. When she looked in his direction, his gaze was fixed innocently enough on the sky.

"Come on inside," he invited a moment later. "I promised you coffee. I think Maritza has breakfast ready by now, too."

"Who's Maritza?" Jenny asked.

Her tone suggested a level of distrust that had Janet shooting a warning look in her direction. Harlan, however, appeared oblivious to Jenny's suspicions.

"My housekeeper," he explained. "She's been with the family for years. If you're interested in learning a little Tex-Mex cooking while you're here, she'll be glad to teach you. She's related to Rosa, who owns the Mexican Café in town."

"I hate Tex-Mex," Jenny declared.

"You do not," Janet said, giving Harlan an apologetic smile. "She's a little contrary at this hour."

"Seemed to be that way at midday, too," he stated pointedly. "Not to worry. It would be an understatement to say that I've had a lot of experience with contrariness."

He led the way through the magnificent foyer and into a formal dining room that was practically the size of Janet's entire house. Her eyes widened. "Good heavens, do you actually eat in here by yourself?"

He seemed startled by the question. "Of course. Why?"

"It's just that it's so . . ." She fumbled for the right word.

"Big," Jenny contributed.

"Lonely," Janet said, then regretted it at once. The man didn't need to be reminded that he was a widower and that his sons were no longer living under his roof. He was probably aware of those sad facts every single day of his life.

He didn't seem to take offense, however. He just shrugged. "I'm used to it."

He gestured toward a buffet laden with more cereals, jams, muffins, toast and fruits than Janet had ever seen outside a grocery store.

"Help yourself," he said. "If you'd rather have eggs and bacon, Maritza will fix them for you. She doesn't allow me near the stuff."

"How come?" Jenny asked.

"Cholesterol, fat." He grimaced. "They've taken all the fun out of eating. Next thing you know they'll be feeding us a bunch of pills three times a day and we won't be needing food at all."

"There are egg substitutes," Janet commented.

"Yellow mush," he contradicted.

"And turkey bacon."

He shuddered. "Not a chance."

Janet chuckled at his reaction. "I'm not going to convince you, am I?"

"Depends on how good you are at sweet talk, darlin'."

Her startled gaze flew to his. Those blue eyes were innocent as a baby's. Even so, she knew in her gut, where butterflies were ricocheting wildly, that he had just tossed down a gauntlet of sorts. He was daring her to turn this so-called arrangement they had made for Jenny's punishment into something personal. The temperature in the room rose significantly.

Nothing would happen between them. Janet was adamant about that. She was in Texas to tap into her Native American roots, not to get involved with another white man. She'd tried that once and it had failed, just as her mother's marriage to a white man had ended in disaster exactly as Lone Wolf had apparently predicted when her mother had fled the reservation.

She drew herself up and leveled a look at him that she normally reserved for difficult witnesses in court. "That, *darlin'*, is something you're not likely to find out," she retorted.

Jenny's eyes widened as she listened to the exchange. Janet was very aware of the precise instant when a speculative gleam lit her daughter's intelligent brown eyes. Dear heaven, that was the last thing she needed. Jenny was like a puppy with a sock when she got a notion into her head. If she sensed there were sparks between her mother and Harlan Adams, she'd do everything in her power to see that they flared into a blaze. She'd do it not because she particularly wanted someone to replace her father, but just to see if she could pull it off.

To put a prompt end to any such speculation, Janet forced a perfectly blank expression onto her face as she turned her attention to the man seated opposite her.

"Exactly what will Jenny be doing today?"

"I thought maybe I'd teach her to ride," Harlan replied just as blandly, apparently willing to let that sudden flare of heat between them die down for the moment. "Unless she already knows how."

"Oh, no," Jenny protested.

Janet jumped in to prevent the tantrum she suspected was only seconds away. "She doesn't, but riding doesn't sound much like punishment or work to me."

"She has to be able to get around, if she's going to be much use on a ranch this size," he countered. "I can't go putting her behind the wheel of a truck again, now can I?''

He glanced at his watch, then at Jenny. ''You ready?''

Jenny's chin rose stubbornly. ''Not if you were paying me a hundred bucks an hour,'' she declared.

Janet thought she detected a spark of amusement in his eyes, but his expression remained perfectly neutral.

''You scared of horses?'' he inquired.

Janet watched her daughter, sensing her dilemma. Jenny would rather eat dirt than admit to fear of any sort. At the same time, she had a genuine distrust of horses, based totally on unfamiliarity, not on any dire experience she'd ever had.

''I'm not afraid of anything,'' Jenny informed Harlan stiffly. ''Horses are dirty and smelly and big. I don't choose to be around them.''

Harlan chuckled at the haughty dismissal. ''I can't do much about their size, but I can flat-out guarantee they won't be dirty or smelly by the time you're finished grooming them.''

Jenny turned a beseeching look in Janet's direction. ''Mom!''

''He's the boss,'' Janet reminded her.

''I don't see you getting anywhere near a smelly old horse,'' Jenny complained.

''You'd be welcome, if you'd care to join us,'' Harlan said a little too cheerfully.

''Perhaps another time. I have to get to work.''

''Why?'' Jenny asked. ''You don't have any clients.''

Janet winced. The remark was true enough, but she didn't want Harlan Adams knowing too much about her law practice, if that's what handling one speeding violation could be called.

"Business slow?" he asked, leveling a penetrating look straight at her.

She shrugged. "You know how it is. I'm new to town."

He looked as if he might be inclined to comment on that, but instead he let it pass. She was grateful to him for not trying to make excuses for neighbors who were slow to trust under the best of conditions. Their biases made them particularly distrustful of a woman lawyer, who was part Comanche, to boot, and openly proud of it.

"What time should I pick Jenny up?" she asked.

"Suppertime's good enough. You finish up at work any earlier, come on out," he said. "We'll go on that ride. I never get tired of looking at the beauty of this land."

Janet found herself smiling at the simplicity of the admission. She could understand his appreciation of his surroundings. Perhaps even more than he could ever guess.

"Maybe I'll take you up on that one of these days," she agreed. She stood and brushed a kiss across her daughter's forehead. "Have a good time, sweetie."

"Is that another one of those things you tell all your clients who end up in prison?" Jenny inquired, her expression sour.

"You're not in prison," Janet observed, avoiding Harlan's gaze. She had a feeling he was close to laughing and exchanging a look with her would guarantee it. Jenny would resent being laughed at more than anything.

"Seems that way to me," Jenny said.

"Remind me to show you what a real prison looks like one of these days," Janet countered. "You'll be grateful to Mr. Adams for not sending you to one."

Janet decided that was as good an exit line as she was likely to make. She was halfway to the front door when she realized that Harlan had followed her. He put his hand on her shoulder and squeezed lightly.

"She'll be okay," he promised.

Janet grinned at his solemn expression. "I know," she agreed. "But will you?"

Chapter Three

When Janet's car had disappeared from sight, Harlan turned and walked slowly back inside. For the first time he was forced to admit that his decision to haul Jenny Runningbear's butt out to White Pines to work off her debt wasn't entirely altruistic. He'd wanted to guarantee himself the chance to spend more time with her mother.

But now, with Janet on her way back to town and her taunt about his ability to manage Jenny ringing in his ears, he wondered precisely what he'd gotten himself into.

Raising four stubborn sons, when he'd had authority and respect on his side, had been tricky enough. He had neither of those things going for him now. If anything, Jenny resented him and she had no qualms at all about letting him know it.

He sighed as he stood in the doorway to the dining room and studied Jenny's sullen expression. If ever a teen had needed a stern hand, this one did. Whether she knew it or not, she was just aching for someone besides her mama to set some rules and make her stick to them.

It was a job her father should have been handling, but he'd clearly abandoned it. It was little wonder the girl was misbehaving, he thought with a deep sense of pity. Typically in the aftermath of divorce, she was crying out for attention. Maybe she'd even hoped if she were difficult enough, she'd be sent back to her father for disciplining.

It took some determination, but Harlan finally shoved aside his inclination to feel sorry for her. It wouldn't help. He figured whatever happened in the next few minutes would set the tone for the rest of the days Jenny spent at White Pines.

"Thought you'd be outside by now, ready to get to work," he announced. "I won't tolerate slackers working for me."

Her gaze shot to his. "What does this crummy job pay anyway? Minimum wage, I'll bet."

"It pays for a smashed up pickup, period. Think of it as a lump sum payment."

"I'll want to see the repair bill," she informed him. "If the figures for my pay, based on the minimum hourly wage, are higher, I'll expect the rest in cash."

Harlan wanted very badly to chuckle, but he choked back his laughter. This pint-size Donald

Trump wannabe had audacity to spare. "Fair enough," he conceded.

"And I'm not getting on a horse," she reminded him belligerently.

"That's something we can discuss," he agreed. "Meantime, let's get out to the barn and groom them. They've been fed this morning, but tomorrow I'll expect you to do that, too."

She stood slowly, reluctance written all over her face. Harlan deliberately turned his back on her and headed out through the kitchen, winking at Maritza as he passed. He didn't pause to introduce them. He had a feeling Jenny would seize on any delay and drag it out as long as she possibly could. She might even inquire about those Tex-Mex recipes she claimed not to like, if it would keep her out of the barn a little longer.

With her soft heart, Maritza would insist on keeping Jenny in the kitchen so she could teach her a few of her favorite dishes and coddle her while she was at it. That would be the end of any disciplining he planned. Until he'd laid some ground rules and Jenny was following them, he figured he couldn't afford to ease up on her a bit. Her very first day on the job was hardly the time to be cutting her any slack.

"Was that your housekeeper?" Jenny asked, scuffing her sneakers in the dust as she poked along behind him.

"Yes."

"How come you didn't introduce us?"

"No time for that now," he said briskly. "You have a job to do. You'll meet Maritza at lunch. She'll be bringing it out to us."

"We're going to eat in the barn?"

Harlan hid a grin at her horrified tone. "No, I expect we'll be out checking fences by then."

She scowled at him. "I thought you were rich. Don't you have anybody else working this place? I can't do everything, you know. I'm just a kid."

"Trust me, you won't even be scratching the surface. And yes, there are other people working the ranch. Quite a few people, in fact. They report to my son. They're off with the cattle or working the fields where we have grain growing." He shot her a sly look. "You had any experience driving a tractor?"

"The sum total of my entire driving experience was in your truck yesterday," she admitted, then shrugged. "You want to trust me with a tractor after that, it's your problem."

He grinned. "You have a point. We'll stick to horses for the time being."

He led her into the barn, which stabled half a dozen horses he kept purely for pleasure riding. Jenny eyed them all warily from the doorway.

"Come on, gal, get in here," he ordered. "Let me introduce you."

"Isn't it kind of sick to be introducing me to a bunch of horses, when you didn't even let me say hello to the housekeeper?"

"You'll get to know Maritza soon enough. As for these horses, from now on they're going to be your responsibility. I want you getting off on the right foot with them.'' He pulled cubes of sugar from his pocket. ''You can start off by offering them these. That'll get you in their good graces quick enough. Let's start over here with Misty. She's a sweetie.''

Jenny accepted the sugar cubes but she stopped well shy of Misty's stall. ''Why is she bobbing her head up and down like that?''

''She wants some of that sugar.''

Jenny held out all of it. ''Here. She can have it.''

''Not like that,'' he corrected, ''unless you want her to nip off a few fingers at the same time.''

He showed her how to hold out her hand, palm flat, the sugar cube in the middle. Misty took the sugar eagerly. He grinned as Jenny's wary expression eased. ''Was that so bad?''

''I guess not,'' she said, though she still didn't sound entirely convinced.

For the next two hours he taught her to groom the horses, watching with satisfaction as she began first to mutter at them when they didn't stand still for her, then started coaxing and finally praising them as she worked. He'd never known a kid yet who could spend much time around horses and not learn to love them. Jenny's resistance was weakening even faster than he'd hoped.

When he was satisfied that her fear had waned, he walked over to her with bit and saddle. ''How about that ride now? Seems to me like Misty's getting mighty restless and you two seem to have struck up a rapport.''

Jenny regarded the black horse with the white blaze warily. The gentle mare wasn't huge, but Harlan supposed she was big enough to intimidate anyone saddling up for the first time.

"I don't know," Jenny said.

"Let's saddle her up in the paddock and you can climb aboard for a test run. How about that?"

"You're not going to be happy until I fall off one of these creatures and break my neck, are you?" she accused.

"I'm not going to be happy until you try riding one," he countered. "I'd just as soon you didn't fall off and break anything, though I can pretty much guarantee that you'll get thrown sooner or later."

"Oh, jeez," she moaned. "My mom really will sue you if that happens. We'll ask millions and millions for pain and suffering. We'll take this whole big ranch away from you and you'll end up homeless and destitute." The prospect seemed to cheer her.

"I'll take my chances," Harlan said with a grin. "Come on, kid. Watch what I'm doing here. If you don't cinch this saddle just right, you'll be on your butt on the ground faster than either of us would like."

Jenny grudgingly joined him in the paddock. With trepidation clear in every halting move she made, she finally allowed him to boost her into the saddle on Misty's back.

"I don't know about this," she muttered, shooting him an accusing look. "What happens now?"

"I'll lead you around the paddock until you get used to it. Don't worry about Misty. She's placid as can be. She's not going to throw you, unless you rile her."

"Is there anything in particular that riles her?" Jenny inquired, looking down at him anxiously. "I'd hate to do something like that by mistake."

"You won't," he promised.

It only took two turns around the paddock before Jenny's complexion began to lose its pallor. Satisfied by the color in her cheeks that she was growing more confident by the second, Harlan handed her the reins.

Panic flared in her eyes for an instant. "But how do I drive her?"

"You don't *drive* a horse," he corrected. He offered a few simple instructions, then stood by while Jenny tested them. Misty responded to the most subtle movement of the reins or the gentlest touch of Jenny's heels against her sides.

"Everything okay?" he called out as she rode slowly around the paddock.

Jenny turned a beaming smile on him. "I'm riding, aren't I? I'm really riding!"

"I wouldn't let you enter the Kentucky Derby just yet, but yes, indeed, you are really riding."

"Oh, wow!" she said.

Harlan chuckled as she seemed to catch herself and fall silent the instant the words were out of her mouth. Clearly she feared that too much enthusiasm would indicate a softening in her attitude toward this so-called prison sentence she felt had been imposed on her.

"I'm ready to get down now," she said, her tone bland again.

Harlan patiently showed her how to dismount. "I think you're going to be a natural," he said.

She shrugged with studied indifference. "It's no big deal. I'd like to go inside now. Too much sun will give me skin cancer."

He hid another grin. "Run on over to the kitchen. Maritza will give you some suntan lotion. She might even have some of those cookies she was getting ready to bake out of the oven by now."

"Jeez, milk and cookies, how quaint," she grumbled, but she took off toward the house just the same.

"Be back here in fifteen minutes," he shouted after her.

"Slave driver," she muttered.

Harlan shook his head. If she thought that now, he wondered what she'd have to say when she saw the fence he intended for her to learn how to mend.

Janet wasn't sure what to expect when she drove back out to White Pines late that afternoon. She supposed it wouldn't have surprised her all that much to find the ranch in ashes and Jenny standing triumphantly in the circular driveway.

Instead she found her daughter sound asleep in a rocker on the front porch. Harlan was placidly rocking right beside her, sipping on a tall glass of iced tea. He stood when Janet got out of the car and sauntered down to meet her. Her stomach did a little flip-flop as he neared.

To cover the tingly way he managed to make her feel without half trying, Janet nodded toward her daughter. "Looks like you wore her out, after all."

"It took some doing. She's a tough little cookie."

"At least she thinks she is," Janet agreed. She allowed herself a leisurely survey of the man standing in front of her. "You don't appear to be any the worse for wear. You must be a tough cookie, too."

"So they say."

He tucked a hand under her elbow and steered her toward the porch and poured her a glass of tea. Jenny never even blinked at her arrival.

"Business any better today?" Harlan asked only after he was apparently satisfied that her tea was fixed up the way she wanted it.

Rather than answering, Janet took a slow, refreshing sip of the cool drink. It felt heavenly after the hot, dusty drive. Her car's air-conditioning had quit that morning on her way back to town and she hadn't yet figured out where to go to have it fixed. The sole mechanic in Los Piños, a man with the unlikely name of Mule Masters, was apparently on vacation. Had been for months, according to Mabel Hastings over at the drugstore.

"My, but this tastes good," she said, sighing with pure pleasure. "It's hotter than blazes today. I thought I'd swelter before I got back out here."

"What's wrong with your car? No air-conditioning?"

"It quit on me this morning."

"I'll have Cody take a look at it when he comes in," he offered. "He's a whiz with stuff like that."

"That's too much trouble," she protested automatically. For a change, though, she did it without much energy. It seemed foolish to put up too much of a fuss just to declare her independence. That was a habit she'd gotten into around her ex-husband. Weighing her independence against air-conditioning in this heat, there was no real contest. Air-conditioning would win every time.

"Nonsense," Harlan said, dismissing her objections anyway. "It'll give Cody a chance to snoop. He's dying to get a closer look at you, so he can tell his brothers that I've gone and lost my marbles."

Startled, she simply stared at him. "Why would he think a thing like that?"

His gaze drifted over her slowly and with unmistakable intent. "Because I'm just crazy enough to think about courting a woman like you."

Janet swallowed hard at the blunt response. She could feel his eyes burning into her as he waited patiently for a reaction.

"Harlan, I don't want you to get the wrong idea here," she said eventually.

It was a namby-pamby response if ever she'd heard one, but she'd never been very good at fending off the few men bold enough to ignore all the warning signals she tried to send out. She'd ended up married to Barry Randall because he'd been persistent and attentive . . . until the challenge wore off.

With that lesson behind her, she should be shooting down a man like Harlan Adams with both barrels. Suggesting he might be getting the wrong idea hardly constituted a whimper of protest.

He reached over and patted her hand consolingly, then winked. "Darlin', there is absolutely nothing wrong with the ideas I have. You'll have to trust me on that."

That, of course, was the problem. She didn't trust him or, for that matter, herself. She had a feeling a man with Harlan's confidence and determination could derail her plans for her life in the blink of an eye. She couldn't allow that to happen for a second time.

"You running scared?" he inquired, his lips twitching with amusement.

"Scared? Not me."

His grin broadened. "You sound like Jenny now. I didn't much believe her, either."

"Harlan—"

"Maybe we'd better get this conversation back on safer ground for the moment," he suggested. "Wouldn't want you getting too jittery to drive home tonight. Now, tell me about your day. You never said how business was."

Janet's head was reeling from the quick change of topic and the innuendos Harlan tossed around like confetti. With some effort, she forced her mind off of his provocative teasing and onto that safer ground he'd offered.

"I had a call from somebody interested in having me draw up a will," she told him. "They decided I was too expensive."

"Are you?"

"If I lowered my rates much more, I'd be doing the work for free, which is apparently what they hoped for. The man seemed to assume that since I'm Native American, I handle pro bono work only and he might as well get in on the 'gravy train,' as he put it."

Harlan's gaze sharpened. "You get much of that?" he asked.

He said it with a fierce undertone that suggested he didn't much like what he was hearing. Janet shivered at the thought of what Harlan Adams might do to protect and defend those he cared about.

"Some," she admitted. "I haven't been around long enough to get much."

"Maybe it's time I steered a little business your way."

She suspected that was an understated way of saying he'd butt a few heads together if he had to. She understood enough about small towns to know that a sign of approval from a man like Harlan would guarantee more clients coming her way. As much as the idea appealed to her, she felt she had to turn it down. Barry had always held it over her head that her career had taken off in New York because of his contacts, not the reputation she had struggled to build all on her own.

"No," she insisted with what she considered to be sufficient force to make her point even to a man as stubborn as Harlan appeared to be. "I need to make it on my own. That's the only way people will have any respect for me. It's the only way I'll have any respect for myself."

"Noble sentiments, but it won't put food on the table."

"Jenny and I won't starve. I did quite well in New York. My savings will carry us for a long time."

"If your practice was thriving there, why'd you come here?" Harlan asked.

"Good question," Jenny chimed in in a sleepy, disgruntled tone.

"You know the answer to that," she told her daughter quietly.

"But I don't," Harlan said. "If it's none of my business, just tell me so."

"Would that stop you from poking and prodding until you get an answer?"

"Probably not," he conceded. "But I can be a patient man, when I have to be."

Janet doubted that. It was easier just to come clean with the truth, or part of it at least. "My divorce wasn't pleasant. New York's getting more and more difficult to live in every day. I wanted a simpler way of life."

She shot a look at Jenny, daring her to contradict the reply she'd given. Her daughter just rolled her eyes. Harlan appeared willing to accept the response at face value.

"Makes sense," he said, studying her with that penetrating look that made it appear he could see straight through her. "As far as it goes." He grinned. "But, like I said, I can wait for the rest."

Before she could think of a thing to say to that, a tall, lanky cowboy strolled up. He looked exactly like Harlan must have twenty or so years before, including that flash of humor that sparkled in his eyes as he surveyed the gathering on the porch.

"Looks right cozy," he commented, his amused gaze fixed on his father. "Anything going on here I should know about?"

"Watch your mouth," Harlan ordered. "Janet and Jenny, this tactless scoundrel is my youngest, Cody. Son, this is Janet Runningbear and her daughter Jenny."

Cody winked at Jenny, who was regarding him with blatant fascination. "Don't tell Daddy, but just so you know, I'm the brains behind White Pines."

"If that were true, you'd have better control over your manners," Harlan retorted.

Janet chuckled listening to the two of them. Talk about a chip off the old block. There wasn't a doubt in her mind that any trait Cody possessed, he had learned it at his father's knee. That included everything from charm to arrogance. Still, she couldn't help responding to that infectious grin and the teasing glint in his eyes as he squared off against Harlan. The squabbles around here must have been doozies.

"Why don't you make yourself useful?" Harlan suggested. "Janet says the air conditioner in her car has gone on the blink. Do you have time to take a look at it?"

"Sure thing," Cody said readily. "Let me get a beer and I'll get right on it."

"I could get the beer," Jenny piped up eagerly.

Cody tipped his hat. "Thanks."

Janet speared her daughter with a warning look, then said to Cody, "If one single ounce of that beer is missing when it gets to you, I'd like to know about it."

"Yes, ma'am," Cody said, winking at Jenny, who blushed furiously.

When they were gone, Janet turned to Harlan. "If he were giving the orders, I suspect Jenny would be docile as a lamb the rest of the summer."

"But he's not," Harlan said tersely. "I am."

"Jealous of the impact your son has on the Runningbear women?" she inquired lightly, just to see if the remark would inspire the kind of reaction she suspected it would.

Harlan's expression did, indeed, turn very grim. "He's married."

She grinned. "I know. Heck, everyone in town heard about his courting of Melissa Horton. It was still fresh on their minds when I moved here. But last I heard, looking's never been against the law. I ought to know. I read those big, thick volumes of statutes cover-to-cover in school."

He scowled. "You deliberately trying to rile me?"

"I didn't know I could," she declared innocently.

"Well, now you know," he asserted.

Janet couldn't help feeling a certain sense of feminine satisfaction over the revelation. But hard on the heels of that reaction came the alarm bells. It was entirely possibly that she was enjoying taunting Harlan Adams just a little too much. She had a hunch it was a very dangerous game to play. He struck her as the kind of man who played his games for keeps.

Chapter Four

Harlan hadn't liked the gut-deep jealousy that had slammed through him when he'd seen the amused, conspiratorial look Janet and Cody had exchanged. Her comment that checking a man out wasn't any sort of legal sin had grated on his nerves just as badly.

Even though he'd guessed that the woman was deliberately baiting him, his blood had simmered and his temper had bordered on exploding. It was an interesting turn of events. He hadn't expected to react so strongly to a woman ever again.

Oh, he'd been attracted to Janet Runningbear the moment he'd set eyes on her. He'd been convinced, though, that he'd deliberately set out to settle her into a corner of his life just to relieve the boredom with an occasional feisty exchange. She was doing that, all right, and more. In spades.

She was stirring up emotions he'd thought had died the day he'd buried his wife just over a year ago. He wasn't so sure he wanted that kind of turmoil.

Unfortunately, he was equally uncertain whether he had any choice in the matter. It had been his observation that when a man was hit by a bolt of lightning—literally or in the lovestruck sense of the phrase—there was no point in trying to get out of the way after the fact.

Given all that, he was almost relieved when Cody announced that the car's air conditioner was working. Janet declined a halfhearted invitation to stay for supper, insisting that she and Jenny had to get home. Harlan waved them off with no more than a distracted reminder to be there at dawn again.

"Well, well, well," Cody muttered beside him.

Harlan frowned at his son's knowing expression. "What's that supposed to mean?"

"Just that it's downright interesting to watch a woman twist you this way and that without even trying."

"I don't know what you're talking about."

Cody grinned. "Then you're in an even more pitiful state of denial than I imagined. Want me to call in Jordan and Luke? Among us we probably have enough experience with women to give you any advice you need. Goodness knows we denied our feelings long enough to drive just about everyone around us to distraction. No sense in you doing the same thing, when we can save you all that time."

"Go away."

"Not till I'm through watching the entertainment," Cody shot back as he sauntered over to his pickup. "'Night, Daddy. Sweet dreams."

Sweet? Harlan could think of a dozen or more words to describe the kind of dreams Janet Runningbear inspired and "sweet" would be very low on the list. Provocative. Seductive. Steamy. Erotic. He had to go inside the air-conditioned house just to cool off from the images.

He consoled himself with the possibility that their first two meetings might have been aberrations. Boredom could play funny tricks on a man. The first thing that came along to relieve it might get exaggerated in importance.

Yes, indeed, that had to be it, he decided as he settled into a chair in his office with a book he'd been wanting to read for some time. A good, page-turning thriller was exactly what he needed tonight. That ought to get his juices flowing better than a leggy, sassy woman.

But the words swam in front of his eyes. His thoughts kept drifting to the enigmatic woman who presented such a placid, reserved facade. He'd enjoyed sparking confusion in those dark, mysterious eyes. He'd relished making a little color climb into her cheeks. Janet Runningbear wasn't nearly as serene around him as she wanted desperately for him to believe.

He also had the feeling, virtually confirmed by her earlier, that there were secrets to be discovered, hidden reasons behind her decision to relocate to Texas.

As a kid he'd been fascinated by stories of buried treasure. He'd spent endless hours searching for arrowheads left behind by Native Americans who'd roamed over the very land on which White Pines had been built. Somewhere in the house, probably in Cody's old room, there was a cigar box filled with such treasures.

If Janet Runningbear had secrets, he would discover them eventually. He'd make a point of it.

And then what? He wasn't the kind of man who courted a woman just for sport. He never had been. He'd tried to instill the same set of values in his sons, tried to teach them never to play games with women who didn't fully understand the rules.

Everything about Janet that he'd seen so far shouted that she was a woman deserving of respect, a single parent struggling to put a new life together for herself and her daughter. If he was only looking for diversion, would it be fair to accomplish it at the expense of a woman like that? It was the one question for which he had an unequivocal answer: no!

So, he resolved, he would tame his natural impatience and take his time with her, measuring his feelings as well as hers. It was the only just way to go.

But even as he reached that carefully thought-out decision, the part of him that leapt to impetuous, self-confident conclusions told him he was just delaying the inevitable. He'd made up his mind the minute he'd walked into her office that he wanted her and nothing—not his common sense, not her resistance—was going to stand in his way for long.

* * *

"Where the devil have you been?" Mule asked in his raspy, cranky voice when Harlan finally got back into town on Saturday after four whole days of trying to keep Jenny Runningbear in line. "Ain't seen you since that gal stole your truck."

Mule's expression turned sly. "Word around town is that you've got her working out at White Pines."

Harlan tilted his chair back on two legs and sipped on the icy mug of beer Rosa had set in front of him the minute he sat down. "Is that what you're doing with your time these days, sitting around gossiping like an old woman?" he asked Mule.

"It's about all there is to do since you dropped out of our regular poker game to play nursemaid to that brat."

Harlan accepted the criticism without comment. Mule grumbled about everything from the weather to politics. His tart remarks about Harlan's perceived defection were pretty much in character and harmless.

Mule's watery hazel eyes narrowed. "I don't hear you arguing none."

"What would be the point? You think you know everything there is to know about the situation."

"Meaning, you think I don't, I suppose. Okay, so fill me in. Why'd you hire her?"

"Because she owes me a lot of money for repairs to my pickup," he said simply. "You ought to know. I had it towed to your garage."

"Ain't had time to take a look at it," Mule said.

"When are you planning to end this so-called vacation of yours?"

"Who says I am? I'm getting so I enjoy having nothing to do. Maybe I'll just retire for good."

Harlan nodded. "You're old enough, that's for sure. What are you now, eighty?"

Mule regarded him with obvious indignation. "Sixty-seven, which you know danged well."

"Of course," he said. "Must be that boredom ages a person, lets his mind go weak."

"There ain't a thing wrong with my mind."

"Then I'd think you'd be itching to tackle a job like that truck of mine."

"I'll get to it one of these days," Mule said. "When I'm of a mind to."

"If you don't plan on going back to work, maybe you ought to sell the garage. The town needs a good mechanic. Cody had to fix Janet Runningbear's air-conditioning the other night, because you're on this so-called extended vacation of yours."

"Bet he ruined it," Mule commented with derision. "Air-conditioning's tricky."

"It's been working ever since," Harlan said, deliberately setting out to goad the old coot into going back to the job he'd loved. "You know Cody has a way with mechanical things. He's probably better than you ever were and he's not even in the business. Maybe I'll have my truck towed out to White Pines and have him take a look at it."

Mule set his beer down with a thump. "I told you I'd get to it."

"When?"

Mule sighed. "First thing on Monday."

"Fair enough."

"Just don't start bugging me about when it'll be done. Decent work takes time and concentration."

Which meant it might take months before he saw that pickup again, Harlan decided. Still, he couldn't regret his decision to have the truck taken to Mule's garage, rather than someplace bigger or fancier in another town.

His friend had closed up shop almost three months ago for no reason Harlan had been able to discern. He'd been on this strike of sorts ever since. He wasn't likely to be happy again until he had his head poked under the hood of a car.

"Don't look now, but that brat is heading this way," Mule announced. "With her mama. Whoo-ee, she sure is a looker, isn't she?"

Harlan tried not to gape as Janet came into Rosa's wearing a vibrant red sundress that bared tanned shoulders and swung loosely around shapely calves. Her straight, shiny hair hung halfway down her back like a shimmering waterfall of black silk. He stood automatically at the sight of her.

"You again?" Jenny greeted him irritably. "This is my day off. I thought I'd get a break. Shouldn't you be mucking out stalls or something? I hope you're not planning to leave 'em untouched all weekend and expect me to clean up the mess on Monday."

He grinned. "It's nice to see you, too," he commented, and winked at her mother. "Even nicer to see you. Care to join us?"

Janet glanced at her daughter's sour expression, then back at him. "I'm not sure that's such a good idea. The company might ruin your appetite."

"I'll take my chances," Harlan said. "By the way, this is Mule Masters."

"The vacationing mechanic," Janet said, smiling at him.

"Not anymore," Mule grumbled, ignoring the hand she held out. Apparently he had more resistance than Harlan did to Janet's dazzling smile.

"He'll be back on the job on Monday," Harlan explained. "Hopefully his manners will improve by then, as well."

"When a car's as old as mine, it pays to know a good mechanic and I hear you're the best around," she said.

Harlan was impressed that she apparently had not taken offense at Mule's deliberate slight. Maybe she'd been able to judge for herself that it wasn't personal. Mule was just a cantankerous old man. Could be, too, that she'd just weighed his manners against her need for a decent mechanic and decided to ignore his grumpiness.

At her praise for his skill, Mule shot Harlan a triumphant look. "Cody couldn't be that danged good, after all, if she's still on the lookout for somebody who knows his business."

"Cody was just doing me a favor," she acknowledged.

"You get what you pay for," Mule noted in a dire tone as Janet and Jenny sat down in the chairs Harlan pulled out for them.

"As you can see, Jenny's not the only one at the table with an attitude," Harlan commented. "I've been putting up with Mule for years, partly because he keeps my cars running, but mostly because he loses regularly at poker.''

"I can play poker," Jenny chimed in. "You guys play for money?"

"Is there any other way to play?" Mule retorted. "Don't play with girls, though."

"Why not?" Jenny demanded. "That sounds like a sexist policy to me. Either open your game to girls or I'll have Mama see that it's closed down."

Mule stared at her in open-mouthed astonishment. Harlan chuckled at the reaction. Jenny had been throwing him off stride the same way all week long.

"Don't play with girls," Mule repeated irritably.

Jenny pulled ten dollars out of her pocket and slapped it on the table. "My money's good."

Janet sighed. "Jenny, that's your allowance for the entire week. If you lose it playing poker, you're out of luck."

Jenny's chin rose a notch. "I don't intend to lose," she declared, leveling a challenging look straight at Mule. "You scared to play me?"

"Dang, but you've got a mouth on you," Mule commented. He glanced at Harlan. "Think we should bring her down a peg or two?"

"No," Harlan said succinctly, his gaze fixed on Janet as he tried to gauge her reaction. "She's already in debt up to her eyeballs."

"That's okay," Janet said. "If she wants to risk her allowance, it's up to her. Of course, I'm going to hate like crazy having to defend all three of you, if you get caught gambling illegally."

"Won't happen," Mule informed her. "Sheriff eats over at DiPasquali's every day. He's sweet on the daughter. Can't budge him out of there for anything less than murder."

Jenny grinned. "All right. Where are the cards?"

Harlan sighed and resigned himself to teaching Janet's rebellious daughter yet another lesson. He glanced into Janet's surprisingly amused eyes. "You in?" he asked her as Mule shuffled the worn deck he'd pulled from his pocket.

"No, I think I'll just sit here and enjoy the competition. I try real hard not to deliberately break the law, even when there's not much chance of getting caught."

"And here I had you pegged for a risk-taker," Harlan taunted.

Color flooded her cheeks. "Depends on the risk and the odds," she snapped right back. "Some are worth taking. Some aren't."

He winked at her. "I'll bet it's going to be downright fascinating figuring out which are which."

She swallowed hard and turned away. "Rosa," she called. "A beer, please."

That choked voice had Harlan smiling. "Throat dry?" he inquired.

"Parched," she admitted, meeting his gaze evenly. She ran her tongue over her lips. "Absolutely parched."

Maybe the gesture was innocent. Maybe not. Harlan doubted he'd ever know for sure. One thing was certain, she could best him at his own game anytime. The sight of that pink tongue delicately sliding over those lush red lips turned his blood hotter than asphalt on a Texas summer afternoon.

It also rattled his concentration so bad that he lost the first hand of poker to Jenny. So did Mule, which suggested that the thirteen-year-old just might know a little more about the game and gambling than he'd suspected.

He glanced up from his second hand to find Janet's gaze fixed on him. She leaned forward, which caused her sundress to dip a provocative inch or so, revealing just enough cleavage to make his own throat go dry.

"Mind if I take a look?" she inquired, placing her hand over his and turning his cards in her direction.

Harlan sucked in a breath as every muscle in his body tightened at that innocent, cool touch. He glanced into her eyes and changed his mind. There was nothing innocent about that touch. She knew exactly what she was doing. He pulled his cards out of her grasp.

"Trying to rattle me, darlin'?" he asked, amused by the blatant tactic.

Her eyes widened. "Why would I do that?"

"Maybe to protect Jenny's allowance," he suggested.

She grinned and shrugged, clearly not the least bit guilty at having been caught. "Hey, us gals have to stick together."

Mule stood, his whole demeanor radiating indignation. "A man would get shot for cheatin' at cards."

Harlan shook his head at his friend's idea of saloon-style justice. "Sit down, old man. I believe Ms.

Runningbear will behave from now on out.'' He met her gaze. ''Isn't that right?''

''I'll be innocent as a lamb,'' she promised. ''Hands on the table. Eyes straight ahead. Lips locked.''

''I can hardly wait to see how long that lasts,'' Harlan commented.

To her credit, she did exactly as she'd sworn she would. Unfortunately for him, she hadn't mentioned a thing about any part of anatomy below her fingertips. Just as he was about to bet, he felt a knee nudge his . . . and stay there. The heat that rose through him this time could have roasted marshmallows. Turned them to ashes, in fact.

He found that he enjoyed the sensation a little too much to tattle on her. He folded and left Jenny and Mule to battle for the pot. Mule took it with a full house to Jenny's two pairs. To his everlasting regret, Janet's knee retreated to a safe distance. It was by far the most intriguing poker game he'd ever played in. So far, it had cost him five bucks.

He considered the money an investment in his future with Janet. He was learning more about her with every hand of cards they played. He doubted she knew how much she was revealing about herself. Maybe she was a risk-taker. Maybe she wasn't. But she was definitely someone who liked to win.

She was also protective as a mother bear with a cub, where Jenny was concerned. And she had an absolutely fascinating, wild flirtatious streak. Just wondering how far she'd take it made his pulse scramble in a way that was downright disconcerting.

"I really think you ought to ante up," he told her as Jenny shuffled the cards for the third hand. He glanced at her daughter. "Deal your mother in this round."

Janet's expression turned faintly uneasy. "Really, I don't think . . ."

"Humor me," he taunted. "I'll spot you the fifty cents for the pot." He tossed two quarters into the middle of the table.

Jenny paused, waiting for her mother's decision before dealing out the hand.

"Okay," Janet said eventually. "But I haven't had as much practice as Jenny."

Jenny's mouth gaped. "Mom!"

"Quiet, dear. Deal the cards."

Harlan chuckled at the exchange. He had the distinct impression now that everything Jenny knew about poker, she had learned from her mother. It was just one more facet to Janet Runningbear to intrigue him. Apparently she was a bit of a gambler, after all.

She scanned her cards with a practiced eye, tossed two back onto the table and waited for Jenny to replace them. Harlan drew three and wound up with two pairs, but most of his attention was on the woman seated next to him. Her face was an absolutely expressionless mask, a genuine poker face.

Mule bet fifty cents. Harlan met his bet. He wouldn't have dropped out of this hand if they'd been playing for a hundred times that amount.

"That's fifty cents to you, darlin'."

She nodded, not even glancing his way. "Your fifty and fifty more."

Jenny looked from her mother to Harlan and back again. "I'll fold," she said.

"I'm out," Mule concurred, tossing his cards onto the table in apparent disgust.

Janet turned an expectant look on Harlan that had his breath catching in his throat.

"Are you in?" she inquired in a lazy, seductive tone that had him conjuring up images that could have melted concrete.

"You'd better believe it, darlin'. Your fifty and I'll raise you a buck."

"My, my, you are confident," she said, turning to wink at Jenny. "Shall I stay, do you think?"

Jenny grinned. "You can't quit now, Mom. He'll think you're chicken."

"True. We can't have that, can we?" She reached over and plucked five dollars from Jenny's pile of winnings. "I'll repay you in a minute."

Harlan studied her expression before matching the bet. He couldn't tell a thing about whether or not she was bluffing. He dropped his money on the table. "Call."

She placed her first card on the table, an ace of clubs. Her second card was a seven of clubs. Her third, a five of clubs. The fourth was a two of clubs. "Now what do you suppose I have here?" she inquired, lifting her gaze to clash with his.

"Either another club or more audacity than anyone else in Texas," Harlan quipped.

She winked. "Want to go double or nothing on this last card?"

"That ain't the rules," Mule complained.

"Some rules are made to be broken," Harlan said, his gaze never leaving Janet's. "Not double or nothing. How about loser cooks dinner for the winner?"

The flash of uncertainty in her eyes told him she'd just realized that she'd overplayed her hand. Still, she didn't back down.

"You sure that's what you want? You could just quit now," she said, clearly determined to brazen it out.

"Not on your life. Get that card on the table."

She sighed, an expression of resignation on her face as she dropped an ace of hearts on top of the other cards.

Harlan chuckled. "Darlin', you would have made an outstanding stripper," he teased. "You know a heck of a lot about drawing out the suspense."

"But you can beat a pair of aces, can't you?"

He showed her his two pairs, fours and eights. "Sure can. So, when's dinner?" he inquired as he gathered up the pot.

Jenny chuckled. "You still think you won, don't you? Wait till you try Mom's cooking!"

"Jenny," Janet protested. "How's tomorrow? I'm sure I can grill a hamburger or something that will be edible."

"That'll be a first," her daughter retorted. She glanced at Harlan. "You might want to bring along a roll of antacids. Mom's still trying to figure out how to cope with life without takeout."

"I'm sure anything your mother cooks will be just fine," Harlan said staunchly. "I'll be there about six."

Mule cackled. ''Think I'll let the rescue squad know to be standing by just in case.''

They could all joke all they wanted, Harlan thought as he tilted his chair onto its back legs and studied the trio. Even if Janet's food tasted like cinders, he had definitely come out of this a winner.

Chapter Five

The kitchen was in shambles. Janet stood amid the collection of messy bowls, streaks of chocolate cake batter and spatters of frosting and despaired of ever getting a meal on the table by six o'clock.

"Why did you let me do that?" she asked Jenny, who was standing in the doorway gloating. "Why on earth did you let me make a bet like that?"

"You sounded like you were on a roll, Mom. How was I supposed to know you just had a piddly pair of aces?"

"Because you know what a competitor I am. I always get caught up in the moment, start bluffing and get carried away. You were doubling your allowance playing poker with me when you were eight for that very reason."

"I know," Jenny said, grinning. "If you'd gotten any more carried away yesterday, the man would be moving in with us."

"Hardly," Janet denied.

"Mom, it's true. He leveled those baby blues of his on you and you perked up as if he'd showered you with diamonds."

Janet winced at the accuracy of the accusation. She had enjoyed the challenge and the blatant masculine approval she'd been able to stir with a little teasing. Harlan Adams was the kind of man who could make any woman lose sight of her independent streak.

"All women are a little susceptible to flattery and the attention of an attractive man," she said to defend herself. "It's not something to be taken seriously."

"You've got my jailer coming to dinner in twenty minutes and you think that's not serious," Jenny retorted.

"Would you stop calling him that?" she implored. "Mr. Adams did you a favor, young lady. And the truth is, you're having fun at White Pines, aren't you?"

"Oh, sure, I just love spending my summer vacation breaking my back mucking out that stinky old barn."

"You should have thought of that before you stole his truck," she admonished for what must have been the hundredth time.

"How was I supposed to know that pickup belonged to a man who'd never heard of child labor laws? You probably ought to investigate him or something. He probably has little kids all over that ranch of his, working their butts off.'' She shot a sly look at Janet. ''Little Native American kids, Mom.''

Janet chuckled at the blatant attempt to try to push her buttons. ''Forget it, Jenny. You can't rile me up that way. There is absolutely no evidence that anything like that is going on at White Pines.''

''Isn't that why we're here, though? Aren't you supposed to be righting old wrongs, looking out for the descendents of the Comanches who rightfully belong on that land that Mr. Adams's ancestors stole? Jeez, Mom, we're in town for less than a month and you're practically in bed with the enemy.''

''I am not in bed with anybody,'' Janet said. ''Stop with that kind of talk and set the table.''

''Okay, but I say you're selling out.''

''And I say you have a smart mouth. I'd better not hear any of that kind of talk while Mr. Adams is here.''

Jenny nodded, her expression knowing. ''I get it. You don't want to tip him off too soon that his days on that land are numbered, right? You'll finish your research, then *bam,* file the papers and boot him off. That's good. I like it. Boy, will he be surprised when he finds out I belong at White Pines more than he does. Maybe I'll even make *him* clean the barn.''

Janet was beginning to regret ever having told Jenny how the land that Lone Wolf's father had cherished had been taken over by white ranchers, while the Comanches were forced into smaller and smaller areas and eventually out of Texas altogether.

"Sweetie, there is no evidence that White Pines itself belonged to Lone Wolf's father," she explained. "True, he roamed all over west Texas and the Comanches believed that the land of the Comancheria was theirs, but it's not as if it was ever deeded to them and recorded as theirs."

"But that's just a technicality, right?" Jenny argued. "You're going to prove that possession was nine-tenths of the law stuff and that the government never had any right to force them out, right?"

Janet had to admit it was a dream she had had, a fantasy inspired by listening to Lone Wolf spin his sad tales. She had vowed at his grave, when she was younger than Jenny was now, that she would try to rectify what had happened to their ancestors.

When her marriage had failed, she'd been drawn to Texas at least in part to see if there was any way at all to fulfill that old promise. Now, while it seemed likely there was much she could do to assist the scattered Native Americans still living in Texas, reality suggested there was little chance she could return their old lands to them. While principle dictated the claims of the tribe were valid, individually their legal rights were murky at best.

"Jenny, you know that's what I want to do, but it's complicated. I can't just waltz into the courthouse and file a few briefs and expect a hundred years of wrongs to be righted. The system doesn't work that way."

"The system stinks," Jenny retorted, thumping the plates onto the table. "And just remember, Mom, Mr. Adams is part of that system."

Janet sighed. It wasn't something she was likely to forget. If the twinkle in his eyes or the fire stirred by a casual touch distracted her, she had only to gaze around at his land to remember what had brought her to Texas.

Every acre of raw beauty reminded her of Lone Wolf's broken father, forced to live as a farmer in an unfamiliar state when tradition and instinct made him a hunter.

In the abstract, it had been easy to hate the Texans who had made that happen. Now, faced with a man like Harlan Adams, who had shown her nothing but kindness, compassion and a hint of desire, it was awfully hard to think of him—or even his faceless ancestors—as the enemy.

So, what did she consider him to be? she wondered as she checked the cake she had baking. Her mother, a full-blooded Comanche, had barely survived a disastrous marriage to a white man. Janet was only half Comanche and her own marriage to a white man had been only minimally better. She'd convinced herself that returning to Texas to learn more about her Comanche heritage was the secret to happiness.

Was Jenny right? Was she selling out already by allowing Harlan Adams to assume such a significant role in their lives? It was not as if she'd had much choice, she consoled herself. Jenny had gotten their lives entwined from the moment she'd impulsively stolen that truck of his.

As for the way she responded to Harlan's warm glances, that was just hormones talking. Her good sense could overrule that anytime she chose—or so she prayed.

She reached into the oven to remove the cake. The pot holder slipped. Her thumb landed squarely on the pan.

"Damn," she muttered as the round pan clattered to the floor. A crack the size of the Grand Canyon appeared down the middle of the cake. Jenny appeared just in time to stare in dismay at the mess.

"Jeez, Mom, that cake was about the only thing this meal had going for it."

"Don't remind me," she muttered, sucking on her injured thumb. "I'll fill it in with frosting, so it'll look okay. We'll cut pieces from the outside edges. Harlan will never know."

"I don't know. I think after he gets a taste of that limp spaghetti and the wilted salad, he'll be expecting it."

Janet scowled at her daughter. "You're no help. A little encouragement would be welcomed about now."

"You need more than encouragement to bail you out," Jenny declared derisively. "How about a quick trip to DiPasquali's? I could be back before he gets here. He'll never know you didn't prepare every bite yourself."

Janet was sorely tempted to do just that. For some reason that probably didn't bear too close a scrutiny, she really had wanted this meal to go well. She surveyed the mess in the kitchen, then glanced at the clock. He was due in five minutes.

"There's no time," she said, resigned to serving a meal barely fit for human consumption.

"You call. I'll run," Jenny repeated. "If he's here when I get back, I'll slip in through the kitchen. Just keep him out of here."

Janet reached for her purse and pulled out a twenty. "Go," she said. A survey of the disaster she'd made of the kitchen had her adding, "And don't worry about coming in through the kitchen. I wouldn't let Harlan in here if it were burning down and he were the volunteer fireman."

When Jenny was gone and she'd placed the desperation call to Gina DiPasquali, she left the kitchen and closed the door behind her. If there'd been a lock, she would have turned the key.

At least the dining room looked presentable. Jenny had even picked flowers for the center of the table and had put out the good china and silver. For all of her grumbling about Harlan Adams, it appeared she wanted to impress him, as well. Janet was more pleased about that than she cared to admit.

She was just checking her makeup in the hall mirror when the doorbell rang. Precisely at six o'clock, she noted, checking her watch. She wondered if that was an indication of polite promptness or, perhaps, just a little eagerness. Her heart thumped unsteadily at the possibility that it might be the latter.

When she opened the door, she could barely glimpse Harlan through the huge bouquet of flowers in his arms.

"Did you buy out the florist's entire stock?" she asked, taking them from him.

He shrugged, looking faintly embarrassed. "It was late Saturday. She said it would all spoil by Monday anyway, so she gave me a deal,'' he said, confirming what she'd meant as a facetious comment.

''I see.''

''I brought wine and candy, too. I wasn't sure which you'd prefer.''

''The flowers would have been plenty,'' she assured him, wondering how the devil she was going to keep him out of the kitchen if she took them in there to put them in vases.

He grinned. ''A little over the top, huh?''

''But sweet,'' she assured him.

''It's been a long time since I've gone calling on a lady.''

She could tell. He looked about as at ease as a man making his first trip to a lingerie department. Not even his starched white shirt, expensive black trousers and snakeskin boots could combat the impression made by his anxious expression.

''You seem to forget that this isn't exactly a date,'' she said to reassure him. ''You won dinner fair and square on a bet.''

She waved him toward a chair. ''Have a seat and I'll get these in water. What can I bring you to drink when I come back? Wine? A beer? Iced tea?''

''Iced tea sounds good. Why don't we sit on the porch? It's a nice night. Or is dinner just about ready?''

''No, dinner will be a while,'' she said in what had to be the understatement of the decade. However, sitting on the porch was out of the question. He was bound to spot Jenny returning from DiPasquali's. She grasped desperately for an alternative.

"Actually, I hate to do this to you, but my bathroom faucet has been leaking." Even though the tactic grated, she used her most helpless expression on him. "I don't know the first thing about changing a washer. Could you take a look at it?"

He latched onto the request as if she'd thrown him a lifeline. "Just show me the way."

She led him down the narrow hallway to the old-fashioned bathroom, which, thankfully, Jenny had straightened up after her shower. "I bought washers and there are some tools there," she said, pointing.

"I'll have this fixed in no time," he promised, already loosening his collar and rolling up his sleeves. "By the way, it's nice to walk into a house and smell dinner cooking. There's nothing like the scent of chocolate to make a man's mouth water." He glanced at her and winked. "Unless it's that sexy perfume you're wearing."

"I'm not sure it's perfume you're smelling," she said. "It's probably all these flowers."

He shook his head. "They were in the car with me all the way into town. That's not it. I'd say you're wearing something light with just a hint of spice. It's the kind of thing that could drive a man wild."

Janet could feel herself blushing. "Thanks. If you'll excuse me, I'll get these into water."

In the kitchen she put the flowers down on the only clear surface, the top of the stove, and drew in a deep breath. She hadn't realized what a sucker she was for charm. Maybe it was just the sweetly tentative way in which it was delivered.

She didn't doubt for an instant that Harlan Adams had always been a flirt, but she was also very aware that he was out of practice delivering compliments with all sorts of subtle innuendo behind them. Teasing a woman just to make her feel good was one thing. It was another to be experimenting with dating after so many years of marriage. It made what they were doing here tonight seem riskier and more significant for both of them.

She sighed and forced her attention to the flowers. It took three large vases to handle all of them. She scattered the arrangements around the living room, poured Harlan's iced tea, then traipsed back to the bathroom where she'd left him.

"I brought your tea," she said, keeping one ear attuned to any sounds from the kitchen that might indicate that Jenny had returned. "How's it going?"

"The washer's replaced," he said, his voice muffled. He had his head poked into the vanity under the sink. "Thought I'd check to make sure all the joints were sealed under here while I was at it."

He slid out and grinned at her. "No leaks under there."

She took one look at the streaks of grime on his face and shirt and winced. "Harlan, you're a mess. I'm sorry. I should never have asked you to do this for me, especially when you were all dressed up."

"Stop fussing. A little dirt never hurt anybody. I'll wash up."

"But your shirt..." she protested.

"It's not a problem," he insisted. He shot her a wicked grin. "Unless, of course, you object to a man coming to the dinner table looking like this. I could strip down and let you wash the shirt here and now.''

He seemed a little too eager for her to grab at that solution. ''Never mind,'' she assured him. ''I'm the one responsible. I can hardly complain, can I?''

Just then she heard the kitchen door slam. She plastered what she hoped was an innocent expression on her face. ''Oh, good, that must be Jenny. She's been out for a bit. Now that she's back, I'll get dinner on the table. Go on out to the porch after you've washed up, why don't you? Relax for a minute. I'll call you when everything's on the table.''

''I could help,'' he offered.

''No, indeed. You've done more than enough. Besides, you won the bet. I can't have you helping.''

She took off, trying to ignore the fact that there was something a little too knowing about his expression. He couldn't possibly have guessed what she'd done, could he? No, of course not. As long he remained far away from that kitchen, there was no way he could figure out that she hadn't prepared every dish herself.

Jenny was pulling aluminum pans of food out of paper bags when Janet got back to the kitchen.

''Gina said to warm the lasagna again for a few minutes before you serve it. I've already turned the oven on low. The salad's in that package. She put the dressing on the side, so you could toss it in your bowl.'' She reached into another bag and pulled out a loaf of Italian bread wrapped in foil. ''Garlic bread. It goes in the oven, too.''

Janet rolled her eyes at Jenny's instructions. "I could have figured that much out for myself."

"Who would guess?" Jenny quipped. "So how'd you keep Mr. Adams out of here?"

"I had him fixing the leak in the bathroom."

Jenny grinned. "Good for you. It's about time he sees what it's like to work for free."

"I don't think he thought of it quite that way. He was doing me a favor." She pointed to the bowl of frosting. "The cake should be cool enough by now. You ice it while I toss the salad."

Twenty minutes later they were seated in the dining room. Janet's heart was in her throat as Harlan took his first bite of salad. Would he be able to tell she hadn't prepared it? It was only lettuce, tomatoes and a few radishes. Surely he wouldn't suspect that even that much had been beyond her skill.

"Delicious," he said. "Jenny, I think you sold your mother short when you said she couldn't cook."

Janet shot a warning look at her daughter. Jenny shrugged.

"It's pretty hard to ruin a bunch of lettuce and some tomatoes," she retorted, avoiding Janet's gaze.

The lasagna was an equally big hit. "Can't think when I've had any better," Harlan enthused. "It's every bit as good as Gina DiPasquali's."

Janet groaned and covered her face. There wasn't a doubt in her mind that the jig was up. "You know, don't you?"

"Know what?" Harlan replied, trying to sound innocent and failing miserably.

"That Jenny picked up the salad, bread and lasagna from DiPasquali's."

He winked at Jenny. "Did she now?"

"How did you know?" Janet demanded.

"Saw her running in the front door of the restaurant as I drove through town," he finally admitted as Jenny chuckled.

Janet glared at the pair of them. "And you let me wriggle on the hook like a big old fish. Did you enjoy watching me squirm trying to keep you away from the front of the house till she got back?"

He nodded. "Sure did." He reached across the table and patted her hand consolingly. "That's okay, darlin'. I appreciate you going to all that trouble to impress me."

Janet moaned. "I did not do it to impress you," she declared adamantly.

"She did it to keep you from getting food poisoning," Jenny chimed in. "You should see—"

"That's enough, Jenny," Janet said sharply. She was determined to get through the rest of the evening with some dignity intact. If she wasn't careful, Jenny would be offering Harlan a tour of the kitchen.

"That chocolate cake sure does smell good," he said. "I know Gina didn't stop by and bake that."

"It's got a great big crack right down the middle," Jenny revealed. "I had to patch it together with icing."

Janet scowled at her. "Thank you for sharing that," she grumbled.

Harlan winked at her this time. "Don't fret, darlin'. With chocolate cake, it's taste, not looks, that count."

"I wouldn't hold your breath on that score, either," Jenny warned. "She probably left out something important."

If she could have, Janet would have sent Jenny to her room on the spot before she made any more embarrassing revelations. Unfortunately, she could see the injustice of such an act. She was just going to have to survive this debacle and hope that Harlan wasn't one to gossip. Fortunately, she was in town to practice law, not to do catering.

As it turned out, the cake was not only edible, but actually pretty good. At least Harlan ate two slices of it, his amused gaze fixed on her the whole time. He seemed especially fond of the inch-thick icing in the middle.

The minute dinner was over he shooed Jenny off by declaring that he would help clean up. Jenny didn't have to be asked twice. She was gone before Janet could protest.

"You cannot walk into that kitchen," she said adamantly, though short of stretching out her arms and trying to bar the doorway, she didn't know what she could do to stop him.

He ignored her, picked up an armload of dishes and headed across the dining room. "The sooner we get things squared away in there, the sooner you and I can sit on that front porch and enjoy the breeze."

To his credit, he didn't even blink as he walked into the midst of the mess she'd created trying to make dinner. Maybe he'd served time on KP in the military at some point, she decided as she watched the ease with which he set things right.

"Come here," he commanded when he'd washed the last dish and wiped down the countertops.

"I don't think so," she said, holding up the last plate she was drying as if to ward him off.

He grinned, shrugged and came to her. Before she realized his intentions, he slid his arms around her waist and held her in a loose embrace. "Thank you," he said softly, his breath fanning intimately across her cheek.

"For what?" she asked shakily. Her breath snagged in her throat as she met his gaze.

"For going to so much trouble."

"I told you—"

He reached up and brushed a strand of hair away from her eyes. "I know what you told me, but the fact is you could have served me whatever that was you cooked in the first place and tried to scare me off for good. Instead, you went to a lot of trouble that wasn't necessary. I don't scare that easily."

She sighed. "That's what I'm afraid of."

He studied her intently. The spark of mischief in his eyes raised goose bumps.

"You gonna fall apart if I kiss you?" he inquired.

An unwilling smile tugged at her lips. "I might."

He nodded. "I think I'll risk it anyway," he said softly.

He lowered his head until his lips were a tantalizing hairbreadth above hers. She trembled as she waited for him to close that infinitesimal distance.

When, at last, their mouths met, she could have sworn fireworks exploded. She'd been expecting a kiss that was gentle and tentative. Instead, he plundered, claiming her mouth as surely as his ancestors had claimed Comanche land.

After the first startled instant, when she couldn't have moved if her life depended on it, Janet slid her hands from his shoulders into his thick hair, holding him, encouraging him to continue the assault that had her senses vibrantly, thrillingly alive for perhaps the first time ever. Nothing she had shared with her ex-husband compared to the consuming, white-hot fire raging through her just from Harlan Adams's incomparable kiss.

She willed it to go on forever, imagining all of the wicked places it could take her. But just as she was indulging in sensations so sweet her heart ached for them to continue, she heard a startled gasp behind her.

"Mom, how could you?" Jenny protested with all of the hurt and confusion a thirteen-year-old could experience.

The kitchen door rattled on its hinges as Jenny left far more noisily than she had entered.

"I'll go after her," Harlan offered, but Janet stilled him.

"No, it's up to me. You'd better leave, though. She won't want to see you again tonight and this could take a while."

He nodded, reluctance clearly written all over his face. "If you're sure."

"I am. I'll handle it."

"You'll be at White Pines in the morning, then?"

"That might be difficult," Janet said. "She might not want to be there after this."

"A deal's a deal," he reminded her, his expression intractable.

She saw then, what she should have recognized before. Harlan Adams had a will of iron when it came to the things he wanted. What worried her was that she'd just had unmistakable evidence that what he wanted was her.

Chapter Six

Harlan was up before dawn the morning following his dinner with Janet and Jenny. By six he was pacing the front porch from end to end, wondering if they would show up and if they did, what kind of reception he might get.

He'd cursed himself a dozen different ways on the drive home the night before. As much as he'd been aching to kiss Janet, he never should have taken a chance on doing it where Jenny could walk in on them. Even a fool would have been smarter than that.

Now, not only had he put his relationship with the intriguing Janet Runningbear at risk, but it seemed likely he'd spoiled the fragile rapport he'd been building with her daughter.

When he finally heard the sound of an engine in the distance, his spirits soared, then crashed just as quickly when he saw that it was Cody's red pickup barreling down the lane.

Just what he needed. He doubted there was a chance in hell he could keep his perceptive son from guessing what was on his mind. And if Cody picked up on his mood, he'd be offering unsolicited advice to the lovelorn and enjoying every minute of it.

"Aren't you supposed to be up north today, checking those fence lines?" Harlan grumbled as Cody approached. "You're getting a mighty late start."

Cody eyed him warily. "You roll out on the wrong side of the bed, Daddy?"

"No, it's just that we could lose a lot of the herd if that fence doesn't get taken care of. I shouldn't have to be telling you a thing like that."

"I'm aware of what's at stake," Cody retorted as carefully as if he'd unwittingly walked into a mine field. "Which is why I sent Mac and Luis up there first thing yesterday morning. I didn't want to wait for today."

"Oh," Harlan said, and fell silent. It took everything in him, but he kept his gaze averted from the lane.

"How's Melissa?" he asked eventually since his son didn't seem inclined to venture any further conversation. He couldn't say he blamed him, given the reception he'd gotten so far.

"Fine."

"And Sharon Lynn and the baby?"

"Fine. Just about the same as when you saw them in church yesterday morning."

Harlan shrugged. "Never can tell with kids, though."

"True," Cody said, then suddenly chuckled.

Harlan scowled at him. "What's so blasted amusing?"

"You," Cody said. "What's the matter? Haven't they shown up yet?"

"Who?"

"The tax collectors," Cody retorted with heavy sarcasm. He shook his head. "You are so pitiful. I'm talking about Janet and Jenny, of course."

"No, they're not here yet."

Eyes sparkling with pure mischief, Cody added, "Heard you had quite a poker game with them on Saturday."

So the cat was out of the bag, Harlan thought, stifling a desire to groan. "I suppose Mule couldn't wait to report every detail," he said sourly, resigning himself to as much taunting as Cody cared to mete out.

"Actually, I heard about it from Maritza, who heard it from her cousin Rosa, who witnessed it all right there in her very own café." He grinned. "And just so you know, Luke's housekeeper also got the word from cousin Rosa, which means your oldest son knows every detail by now, too. He couldn't wait to check out the story with me."

"Damn, I knew it was a mistake helping that whole darn family to settle in Los Piños," he muttered, regretting the day he'd first hired Consuela, who was now working for Luke, and subsequently her cousin

Maritza, his present housekeeper. He'd even co-signed the loan for Rosa's damned café. So much for loyalty. They apparently hadn't been able to wait to blab his business all over hell and gone. "Don't they have anything better to do than gossip?"

"Guess not," Cody said. "Especially not when the news is so fascinating. So, how was dinner with the loser?"

With the grapevine already abuzz anyway, Harlan didn't bother trying to contain a grin at the memory of the meal that Jenny had snuck in from Di-Pasquali's.

"Fascinating," he attested.

"So why the worried look when I drove up?"

He weighed telling his son the truth or at least part of it. Maybe if he swore him to secrecy with a promise of eternal damnation if he broke his vow, he could chance it. If he didn't talk about what had happened, he'd go plumb stir-crazy.

"This doesn't get repeated, okay? Luke already knows too much. I don't want him and Jordan hovering around here, trying to decide if I'm losing my mind."

"It may not be Luke and Jordan you need to worry about," Cody drawled. "If Jessie and Kelly get wind of it, they'll get matchmaking fever the likes of which west Texas has never seen."

"All the more reason for you to keep your trap shut," Harlan said, shuddering at the prospect of all that meddling. "Can you do it?"

Eyes dancing with renewed mischief, Cody solemnly crossed his heart. "Not a word. I swear it. What happened last night?"

"No guffawing, okay?"

"I wouldn't dream of it."

Harlan was doubtful about that, but he decided to chance it. "Okay, let's just say the evening ended on a more awkward note than I might have preferred."

Cody's mouth gaped. "You made a pass at her?"

He made it sound like Harlan was sixteen and had been trying to get into the drawers of the preacher's daughter. "It wasn't a pass, dammit. It was a kiss."

"Well, I'll be damned. I bet Luke you wouldn't have the guts to try that for at least another month."

Harlan groaned. "I knew this was a mistake. I knew it." He scowled fiercely. "You blab one word of this and I'll hang your hide from the oak tree out back just to set an example for your brothers."

Unfortunately, Cody didn't exactly seem to be intimidated. He chuckled even as he said, "Not a word. I already promised. Besides, do you think I want Luke to know I lost the bet? So what was so awkward?"

"Jenny walked in."

"Uh-oh."

"Uh-oh is right. She wasn't happy."

"She's a kid. She'll get over it. Surely her mom has been on dates before."

"Maybe. Maybe not. But it took me most of last week to get a civil tongue in that girl's head. Now I've gone and lost whatever ground I gained."

"What was Janet's reaction to all this?"

"Naturally she was upset."

"With you or Jenny?"

"I'm the supposedly responsible adult. I'm the one who caused the problem."

"Not if she kissed you back," Cody corrected. "Did she?"

Harlan couldn't help smiling at the memory. "She did, indeed."

"Then you'll find a way to work it out," Cody predicted, apparently satisfied that he'd completed his role as counselor. "I'm going inside for breakfast. All this advice has left me famished."

"You're always famished," Harlan observed. "Doesn't Melissa ever feed you?"

"Sure, but that was two hours ago," he said as he opened the front door. Just as he was about to step inside, he looked back. "Hey, Daddy?"

Harlan's gaze was already riveted on the lane again. "Hmm?"

"Remember what you used to tell us when we were dating?"

His head snapped around. "What?"

"It's not polite to kiss and tell," Cody taunted.

If he'd had something available, he would have thrown it at him. "Then see that you don't repeat my mistake," he warned emphatically. "There will be hell to pay for both of us, if you do."

By eight o'clock Harlan had just about accepted the fact that Janet and Jenny wouldn't be coming. He decided to let it pass for today, but if they didn't show up tomorrow, he vowed to have a little chat with Jenny about paying off debts and living up to obligations. If he was more concerned about his own selfish interests, well, that was something she wouldn't have to know.

He was in the barn saddling up his favorite stallion when he glanced up to see Jenny standing hesitantly in the doorway. Surprise kept him speechless, even as relief spread through him. When he could keep his tone matter-of-fact, he said, "A little late, aren't you?"

"Mother dropped me off on the highway. I had to walk the rest of the way up the lane."

"I see. Whose idea was that?"

Jenny's chin rose a belligerent notch. "Mine."

He would have guessed as much. It was probably her way of keeping him and her mother apart. The fire in her eyes dared him to make anything of it. He clamped a lid on his desire to challenge her. At least she was here. He considered that a good sign.

"The lane's pretty long," he offered blandly. "Must be close to two miles. You thirsty?"

"A little," she admitted, scuffing her sneaker in the dirt and avoiding his gaze.

"Then, run on in the house and have Maritza give you something cool to drink."

She didn't dash off as he'd anticipated she would.

"Are you going riding?" she asked.

He nodded. "I was about to."

"Can I come?"

"Of course."

"You'll wait?"

"I'll wait," he agreed, trying to remain as nonchalant as she was when he was filled with questions

about what had happened after he'd left last night.
Her odd mood wasn't telling him much, but at least
she didn't appear to be holding that kiss against him.
She simply appeared determined to stave off a repeat.

"I'll hurry," she promised, and took off.

He stared after her, confusion teeming inside.
Would he ever figure out the workings of that girl's
mind?

Jenny was polite, but quiet for the rest of the day.
She did everything he asked of her, if not eagerly, at
least without complaint. By the end of the day he was
longing for a little of the more familiar sass.

"Is your mama picking you up at the house or are
you meeting her out by the highway?" he inquired
eventually.

"At the highway," she said, shooting a belligerent
look at him that confirmed his earlier opinion that
this was her way of keeping him and Janet sepa-
rated.

"You'd better get going then. It'll take you a while
to get out there. The humidity's up. Maybe you'd
better borrow a baseball cap and get a thermos of
water to take along," he said, deliberately emphasiz-
ing that the walk would seem even hotter and longer
than it had in the cooler morning air.

He let that sink in for a minute, then added casu-
ally, "Or I could drive you out."

He could tell from her expression that she was
struggling with the offer, weighing the advantages of
the quick, cool ride with the disadvantages of having
him possibly bump into her mother.

"I suppose that would be okay," she conceded grudgingly. "I don't want to get heatstroke."

"Good thinking," he said. He glanced at his watch. "Should we leave now? It's almost five."

She nodded and followed him to his car, a luxury model he kept in the garage. Her mouth dropped open when she saw it. "How come you drove that pickup, when you had this?"

"It was more practical. I'm always hauling stuff for the ranch."

"Oh." She touched the leather interior almost reverently. "I like this. It's really soft. I'm going to have a car just like this someday."

"I'll bet you will," he agreed. "Are you planning to earn it or steal it?"

"Hey, that's not fair," she protested, frowning. "I'm really not a thief."

"You couldn't prove that by me."

She grimaced. "It's not like I have a criminal record or something. What happened was just like an impulse or something. The truck was there. I could see the keys inside. I took it. I figured it served you right for leaving the keys inside."

He nodded, hiding a grin. It was a bad habit he and all of his sons had. Half of Los Piños was aware of their reckless pattern. This was the first time, though, that anyone had taken advantage of them.

"I suppose it did," he admitted.

She shot a look at him. "Does that mean I'm off the hook?"

"Not on your life. Even if I'd gone off and left it sitting wide open with the engine running, it wouldn't give you the right to take what's not yours."

"Oh." She looked more resigned that surprised.

At the end of the lane she started to climb out of the car. "It's awful hot out there," Harlan observed. "Not much shade, either. Why don't I wait? You can sit in the air-conditioning."

She promptly shook her head. "I'll be okay. Mom ought to be here any minute."

"What if she got held up?"

"By what? A traffic jam?" she asked sarcastically.

"Maybe a client," Harlan said.

"Yeah, right."

"You never know."

"Oh, for Pete's sake, if you want to wait, wait." She closed the door, settled back in the seat and folded her arms around her middle, her gaze directed out the passenger window toward town.

"You want to talk about it?" he asked eventually.

"About what?"

"What you saw last night?"

"No," she said succinctly.

Harlan weighed everything he knew about raising kids and decided once more to let it pass for now. Let Janet hash it out with her first. If they couldn't settle it, then he'd step in and try to clarify what that kiss had been about . . . assuming he had it figured out by then.

"There she is," Jenny announced, flinging open the car door. "See you."

Her quick flight precluded any opportunity for him to exchange so much as a word with Janet. He rolled down his window and managed a wave that was returned halfheartedly before the car backed onto the highway and disappeared from view as quickly as it had come.

He chafed at letting a thirteen-year-old interfere in his life. He figured Janet ought to be mad as hell about it, too, but she seemed to have accepted Jenny's right to stand squarely between her and him.

For the rest of the week he only managed to eke out bits and pieces of information about Janet from her sullen, tight-lipped daughter. He couldn't seem to break the pattern that had been established on Monday. Janet never came any closer than the end of the lane. Her aloof behavior left him rattled and irritable.

He couldn't recall the last time he'd been so fascinated by a woman. It must have been when he'd first met Mary, though. Not once in all the years since then had he ever strayed in thought or deed.

Mary had been a good wife, devoted to a fault. Sometimes he'd almost regretted the way she'd doted on him to the exclusion of their sons. He'd never doubted her love for Luke, Erik, Jordan and Cody, but she'd focused all of her attention on him. He'd felt cherished and, in return, he had made her the center of his life, as well.

Ever since her death, there had been this huge, empty space inside him. And, despite the attempts of his sons to fill the endless hours of the day, he'd been lonely. He hadn't really recognized that until he'd suddenly felt so alive the minute he'd walked into Janet Runningbear's office after that heart-in-his-throat spectacle of her daughter crashing his pickup into a tree. He wasn't going to give up the feeling she stirred in him without a fight.

By Friday he was at his wit's end. He figured the only way to get back on speaking terms with Janet was to get her clear up to the house. And the only way to do that was to see to it Jenny wasn't waiting at the end of that lane for her.

On Friday morning he enlisted Cody's help. "How about taking Jenny with you this afternoon? It's about time she got a real look at the workings of this place."

If Cody guessed his father's intentions, he didn't let on. "I won't be back until dark," he warned.

"That's okay."

"Won't Janet be expecting to pick her up at five as usual?"

"I'll keep Janet entertained."

Cody grinned. "If you say so. I'll come back for Jenny at lunchtime."

"Thanks, son."

"Don't mention it."

Jenny rode off with Cody just after noon, looking as besotted as if she'd just been granted a date with her favorite movie star. Harlan spent the next few hours catching up on paperwork in his office, then dressed for his meeting with Janet as eagerly as if they were going out on a date. His sons would have laughed their fool heads off if they'd seen him debating what to wear, only to end up in a pin-striped dress shirt with the sleeves rolled up, jeans and his best boots. A pile of discards worse than any Mary had ever left strewn around covered the king-size bed.

Promptly at five he took a pitcher of iced tea, two tall glasses, a bowl of Maritza's *pico de gallo* and some tortilla chips onto the porch. Leaning back in a rocker, his boots propped on the porch railing, he settled back to wait. He wondered how long it would be before Janet guessed that he wasn't bringing Jenny to the end of the lane and resigned herself to driving to the house to pick her up. He figured fifteen minutes.

He was off by five. At ten minutes past five she came flying up the lane, sending up a cloud of dust. She leapt out of the car, her expression half frantic.

"Where's Jenny? Has something happened to her?"

"She's fine," he soothed. "She's off helping Cody this afternoon. She won't be back for a while yet. Come on up and join me."

Janet regarded the tea and tortilla chips suspiciously. "What's all that?"

"Just a little something to tide us over while we wait. Figured you might be thirsty and hungry this time of day."

"Exactly when are you expecting them back?"

"Seven or so."

She stared at him incredulously. "Seven? Why didn't you tell me?"

"I just did," he said, holding out the glass of tea.

Janet ignored it. Hands on hips, she stared him down, practically quivering with indignation. "What kind of game are you playing, Harlan Adams?"

"I could ask you the same question. You've spent the past five days avoiding me. Whose idea was that? Yours or Jenny's?"

She sighed and sank down onto the top step. She finally accepted the glass of tea and took a long swallow. "A little of both, I suppose."

"Shouldn't you have told me?" he said, mimicking her tone.

"I just did," she said, and chuckled. "I'm sorry."

"No need to be sorry. For a pair of grown-ups we are pretty pathetic, aren't we? Seems to me we should be past resorting to games or letting a teenager rule the way we live our lives."

"We should be," Janet concurred. "It's my fault. I should have insisted on bringing Jenny all the way to the house on Monday, but she was still so upset I gave in and dropped her at the end of the lane. After that, it became a pattern, I suppose. I couldn't seem to break it."

"Don't go taking all the blame. I'm the one who put you in an awkward position in the first place." He looked her over, admiring the creamy silk blouse she wore with a pair of tan linen slacks and a few pieces of expensive gold jewelry. She was all class, there was no mistake about that. "You haven't dated much since the divorce, have you?"

"Not at all."

"So Jenny's still very protective. Is she hoping you'll get back together with her father?"

"No, she knows better than that. He doesn't have time for either one of us anymore. I think that's really the problem. She needs all of my attention right now."

Her expression turned speculative. "It may be that she needs all of yours, too. You're providing a father figure for her. Maybe she's not ready to share you."

"But what do you need?" he inquired softly. "Do you need a man in your life?"

She shook her head. "It's not in my plans right now."

He thought of his sons and how hard they'd fought falling in love. In the end, when the right woman came along they hadn't had a choice, any more than he had when he and Mary had met.

"I wasn't aware you could plan for a thing like that," he said.

"You can certainly avoid putting yourself at risk," she countered.

"Is that what you've been doing since you got to Texas, avoiding risks?"

She nodded.

"Must have been a lousy plan, since we met anyway," he observed, grinning. "Or do you suppose fate just had something else in mind?"

"I don't know what to think," she admitted, then gazed at him imploringly. "Harlan, this can't go any further than it already has."

The wistfulness in her voice contradicted the statement and gave him hope. "I think we both know that's not so," he said. "But I'm willing to slow down and take things nice and easy, if that'll give you some peace of mind.''

"Why is it that peace of mind is the last thing I feel around you?'' she asked plaintively.

He winked at her. "Darlin', I think that's exactly what we're going to find out. Now, why don't you and Jenny stick around for dinner? Let's see if we can't get things on an even keel again.''

Janet protested, but she didn't put much *oomph* in it. After seeing her resort to takeout the Sunday before, he could see why. Any meal she didn't have to prepare herself must have seemed like a godsend. Just like any meal he didn't have to eat alone these days was a genuine pleasure for him.

If he had his way about it, there were going to be a whole lot more evenings starting off just like this one.

Chapter Seven

Janet couldn't quite decide whether or not to be irritated at Harlan's high-handedness in sending Jenny off to work with Cody. She knew he had done it just so he could end the stalemate she had started following that devastating kiss.

Jenny's shocked reaction had been partly responsible for her retreat, of course. But it was her own response that had truly shaken her. She wasn't sure she was ready to deal with a man as strong-willed and compelling as Harlan Adams, a man who made her heart pound and her blood sizzle with lust and temper in equal measure. She resented the fact that he had forced her into confronting the issue by facing him again.

Still, once dinner was on the table, her exasperation dwindled at an astonishing rate. Apparently she could be bought for a decent meal she didn't have to cook herself. Tender chicken-fried steak, mashed potatoes and gravy, a salad, vegetables—it was heaven.

Jenny wasn't nearly so easily won over. She sat at the dining room table in stubborn silence, glaring from Janet to Harlan and back again. Apparently she had belatedly guessed that the price of her afternoon with Cody was this unwanted reunion. By the end of the meal Janet's nerves were raw from the tension in the room.

"I think we should go," she said the minute they'd finished dessert. The housekeeper had served a chocolate silk pie that had almost inspired Janet to ask for the recipe until she'd reminded herself what a disaster she'd make of it. "I know eating and running is impolite, but we have things we should be doing."

Harlan regarded her with undisguised amusement. "Such as?"

"Homework," she retorted automatically. "Jenny's doing some make-up assignments so she'll be ready to take advanced English in the fall. She fell behind at the end of the term at home."

"Mom, it's Friday night," Jenny protested, then clamped her mouth shut the instant it apparently dawned on her that speaking out might mean staying at White Pines longer.

Janet hid a smile. "I suppose we could stay a little longer," she said, her expression innocent.

Alarm flared in Jenny's eyes. "No, you're right," Jenny contradicted hurriedly. "I should get my homework done. I have a big project due next week. It'll probably take me hours and hours, maybe the whole weekend. I won't get any sleep at all."

"Sounds like a tough assignment," Harlan agreed. "What is it?"

Jenny looked trapped. "A paper," she finally blurted in a way that said she was ad-libbing as she went along. "On Edgar Allan Poe."

Harlan leaned back. "Ah, yes, Poe. Now there was a writer. Pretty scary stuff, it seemed to me when I read him."

"You read Poe?" Jenny asked in an insulting tone of disbelief that suggested she was surprised to discover that Harlan read at all.

"Poetry, short stories, just about all of it, I suppose," he said, clearly unoffended. "Of course, by today's standards, I suppose he seems pretty tame. Not nearly as graphic as some writers. It always seemed to me there was something to be said for leaving things to the reader's imagination, the way Poe did."

Jenny's expression brightened. "That's what I thought," she said eagerly, then caught herself. "Never mind. You probably don't care about what I think."

Janet's breath caught in her throat as she waited for Harlan's reply. Her ex-husband had never been interested in hearing his daughter's thoughts on much of anything. For the most part, Barry had believed children should be seen and not heard, unless showing Jenny off had had some professional benefit. He'd enjoyed being perceived as an up-and-coming lawyer and proud family man. When Jenny's grades had slipped in direct proportion to the amount of arguing going on at home, he'd lost what little interest he'd ever had in her school days.

For a time, Janet had been fooled by her ex's superficial evidence of concern and pride. Now that she'd observed Harlan Adams for a couple of weeks, especially when Cody was around to banter with him, she had seen what a genuine family was all about. What she and Barry and Jenny had shared had been a mockery of the real thing, more feigned than substantive.

She watched now as Harlan fixed an attentive look on Jenny. That was the gaze Barry had never quite mastered, an expression of real interest. Seeing it warmed Janet through and through and further endangered her already shaky determination to keep Harlan at a distance.

"Of course I'm interested in your opinion," he assured Jenny. "And if you're going to be in an advanced class, you must be pretty smart."

"My teacher in New York said my short stories and essays are really good," Jenny admitted, pride shining in her eyes. "She said I could probably be a writer someday, if I want to be."

"And do you want to be?" Harlan asked.

Jenny nodded, her expression suddenly shy as she revealed a dream that Janet knew she'd shared with almost no one. It was a tribute to the fragile trust flowering between Jenny and Harlan that she was telling him.

Once again, Janet couldn't help thinking that the theft and subsequent accident that had brought Harlan Adams into their lives was turning out far better than she'd had any right to expect, especially for Jenny. It made her more determined than ever not to do anything to shake the trust the two of them were establishing, even if it cost her a chance with Harlan for herself.

"I'm going to write about Native Americans," Jenny said. "I want to tell all the stories that Lone Wolf told Mom."

"And who was Lone Wolf?"

"He was my great-great-grandfather. He died way before I was born."

Harlan glanced at Janet. "But you spent time with him?"

"Just one summer," she admitted sorrowfully. "My father didn't want me spending time with my Comanche relatives. He said I'd grow up wild and out of control. One year, though, my mother insisted. She sent me to stay with Lone Wolf on the reservation in Oklahoma. It was the best summer of my life."

"Which almost explains why you ended up in Texas when your marriage ended," Harlan said. "Why here and not Oklahoma?"

Janet flushed guiltily and avoided Jenny's knowing gaze. "Because he talked about Texas a lot and the days when our ancestors lived here," she said, leaving it at that.

Harlan didn't appear convinced. "Something tells me there's a lot more to it," he said.

"Not really," she denied. "I'm just following a little girl's dream."

He shrugged, finally accepting her at her word. "Then we'll leave it at that for now," he said.

There was no mistaking the implication that he wouldn't leave the topic alone for long. Janet wondered how well her resolve would stand up to any real grilling by this man with the coaxing eyes and persuasive charm.

And more and more she was wondering whether she'd be able to go on battling the warm feelings he was stirring in her, the kind of feelings she'd vowed never to allow to deceive her again.

Harlan Adams struck her as a complicated man of many passions. She could only guess how well she would fare if she became one of them. For her own sake, as well as Jenny's, she hoped the moment of truth would be a long time coming.

"Maybe you should think about spending the weekend here," Harlan suggested just then, startling her. Her panic must have shown because he quickly added, "I've got a whole library filled with works by Poe. Jenny could do all the research she wants right here."

As generous and innocent-sounding as the offer was, Janet was shaking her head before the words were out of his mouth. "No, really, it's impossible. We're not prepared for an overnight stay."

His gaze settled on her in a provocative way that made her pulse race. "The closet's always filled with extra toothbrushes, if that's what has you worried,'' he said.

Janet felt her cheeks flame. He knew precisely what had her worried, and it definitely wasn't toothbrushes or the lack of them. "Thanks for the offer, but no,'' she said firmly.

"Come on back in the morning then,'' he said.

In giving in more gracefully than she'd expected, he almost left her feeling disappointed. Obviously she needed to work a little on her backbone. It was apparently as limp as an overcooked strand of spaghetti.

"Jenny can do her research and you and I could go riding,'' he prodded when she remained silent. "You still haven't seen all of White Pines.''

Janet felt Jenny's wary gaze on her, but she avoided meeting her daughter's eyes. There were a lot of reasons to accept Harlan's offer, beginning with the chance it would give her to explore the very land that her ancestors had once hunted on. Jenny couldn't fault her for that.

There was also one very big reason to turn him down: he made her stomach do the most amazing flip-flops every single time he looked at her. If he could manage that after a few relatively brief encounters, what kind of havoc could he wreak during a whole day's outing? In private? Without Jenny's watchful gaze on them every minute?

Would there be more of those bone-melting kisses like the one that had thrown her so off stride on Sunday night? Without a doubt. The heated promise was in Harlan's gaze every time he looked at her. Temptation heated her blood. Longing made her heart thump unsteadily. And the combination had her saying yes before she could stop herself.

Once the single affirmative word was out of her mouth, Janet wasn't sure which of the three of them was most stunned. A pleased smile hovered on Harlan's lips. Jenny retreated into sullen silence. And Janet considered whether a steel rod implant was necessary to stiffen her spine to the degree it needed.

"Shall we get an early start?" Harlan inquired. "Or are you one of those people who likes to laze in bed on the weekends?"

There was just enough seductive innuendo in the question to make her voice unsteady when she vowed that she could be there at any hour he liked.

He grinned. "Brave words," he taunted. "I'll give you a break just this once, though. You get here by ten. I'll have Maritza pack us a picnic to take along."

"For three," Jenny said, scowling at her mother. "I want to come, too."

"Thought you had a big paper to do," Harlan said, but his eyes were glinting with amusement at Jenny's obvious ploy to play chaperone once again.

"I'll need a break," she said. "Otherwise, my brain will probably bust."

"Then by all means, you'll come, too," he replied. "Can't have a tragedy like that on my head."

If he was disappointed, he didn't let it show. Clearly, he understood how important it was for Jenny to feel she wouldn't be intruding.

For that, Janet decided, he would always have her gratitude. And, if he kept up the sweet gestures and the blatant provocation, he might very well wind up with her heart after all. Only time would tell just how terrible or incredible that fate might be.

Janet Runningbear was skittish as a brand-new colt, Harlan decided midway through their ride on Saturday. He'd never met a woman so determined to avoid being alone with a man.

Of course, Jenny was playing right into her mother's hands by acting like the overprotective adult, rather than the other way around. He might have found it amusing and rather gratifying, if it hadn't been so blasted frustrating.

He wanted to get to know this woman, but whenever he steered the conversation in a personal direction, she scooted it onto some other topic faster than a tornado could rip apart a house. He supposed for the first time in his life he was going to have to learn to be patient. His usual habit of making quick decisions and acting on them wasn't going to work with Janet. If he pushed too hard, he knew right now he'd scare her out of his life entirely.

He kept a close eye on her as they rode. She handled herself well in the saddle. Clearly, this wasn't her first ride on horseback. She didn't bat an eye when he picked up the pace. In fact, she shot him a daring look, dug in her heels and sent the mare he'd chosen for her into a flat-out gallop.

Laughing, Harlan didn't even try to keep up. He was enjoying the view from behind too much. She was leaning low over the horse's back. Her long black hair was caught up in a single, severe braid, but tendrils had escaped to curl defiantly along the back of her elegant, exposed neck. A longing to press a hot, lingering kiss to that bare skin washed through him with the ferocity of a summer storm, stunning him with its intensity.

She slowed after a bit, letting him and Jenny catch up.

"Where'd you learn to ride like that?" he asked. "Not in Central Park, I'll bet."

"Jeez, Mom, you never said you'd been on a horse before," Jenny said, looking a little awestruck.

"I learned in Oklahoma that summer. It all came back to me. I remembered how it felt to have the wind in my face. It's exhilarating."

"It shows," Harlan said quietly, his gaze locked with hers. "You've got some color in your cheeks for a change and your eyes are sparkling."

Jenny shot him a suspicious frown, as if not quite certain whether he was making another pass at her mother right under her eyes.

"It's the God's truth," Harlan insisted with a touch of defiance. "Jenny, take a good look at your mom. Have you ever seen her look so happy?"

Apparently by drawing Jenny into the appraisal of Janet's appearance, he managed to allay her fears. She studied her mother, then nodded. "You do look spectacular, Mom. You should do this more."

"Anytime," Harlan said quickly, capitalizing on the small, inadvertent opening. "No need even to call first. If I'm not around, just leave me a note in the barn or let Maritza know you're taking one of the horses out."

"Thank you," she said, rubbing the mare's neck. "I may take you up on the offer. This has been incredible."

Harlan locked gazes with her once more, refusing to break eye contact as he said, "And it's just the beginning."

Janet swallowed hard under his intense scrutiny. He enjoyed the knowledge that she was responding to him despite whatever reservations she might have. He was finally reassured that this attraction he'd been feeling from the beginning was returned, albeit with great reluctance.

"Come on, you two. I know the perfect spot for our picnic. It's about a mile ahead."

They ambled along at a comfortable pace for the next few minutes, picking their way through a denser stand of trees until they emerged on the shaded bank of a creek. It was too late in the season for the bluebonnets that usually dotted the area, but it was a tranquil, lovely setting just the same. Harlan had always enjoyed coming here when he needed to ponder some puzzle in his life. The serenity seemed to clear his head.

It was also a romantic spot for a picnic. He and Mary had stolen away here a time or two before she'd decided picnics were for youngsters and they needed more sedate and elegant entertainment. He'd always regretted that they no longer shared this spot and the simplicity of the hours they had once spent here.

He kept a close eye on Janet to gauge her reaction. A soft smile lit her face as she took in her surroundings. She sighed then with what looked to be sheer pleasure.

"Lone Wolf used to tell me about incredibly beautiful places just like this," she murmured, lifting her eyes to meet his again. "I dreamed of finding one. Thank you for bringing us here."

As if she sensed that the undercurrents between her mother and Harlan were getting too provocative and too intense, Jenny cut in. "I don't see what's so special. It's just a dumb old creek. I saw the Atlantic Ocean a couple of times when Mom and Dad actually stopped working long enough to take me. Now that's impressive," she said, shooting a defiant look in his direction.

He grinned at her, refusing to take offense. "It is something, isn't it? But appreciating the magnificence of one doesn't mean you can't recognize the beauty of the other. That would be like saying if you like Monet, you can't like Grandma Moses. Or if you enjoy Bach, it's not possible to appreciate the Beatles."

He pointedly fixed his gaze on Janet when he added, "Seems to me the more experiences you open your heart to, the richer your life will be."

Color rose in her cheeks as his implication sank in. Satisfied that she'd gotten his message, he nodded and busied himself with taking the picnic from the packs Maritza had prepared. He handed Janet a red-checked tablecloth.

"You pick the spot for that," he suggested, then watched as she headed unerringly for his favorite place beneath an old cottonwood. It was the exact spot where he often sat, his back braced against the trunk of the tree as he waited for the sun to set and his tangled thoughts to unravel. He'd come a lot after Mary's death, hoping for understanding and acceptance of the tragedy that had taken her.

Today, for the first time, with Janet and Jenny by his side, he thought maybe he'd found the reason for God's choice. One door in his life had closed and another had opened. He couldn't help wondering with a sense of tremendous anticipation what awaited him on this new adventure.

"You suddenly seem very far away," Janet said quietly as she came to stand beside him.

Harlan noticed that Jenny had already stripped off her shoes and socks and was wading in the creek. For the moment he and Janet had a bit of privacy. He lifted his hand to her cheek in a light caress.

"No more," he murmured. "Now I'm right here, with you."

Worry darkened her eyes at once. "Harlan—"

He touched a finger to her lips. "Shh. For once, don't argue. Let's just see where this takes us. No promises. No commitments. No guarantees. Just be open to the possibilities. Can you do that?"

He felt her tremble beneath his touch, felt her skin heat and saw the glitter of excitement in her eyes. A sigh hovered on her lips before she finally nodded.

"I can try," she agreed, looking anything but certain even as she spoke.

"That's all anyone can ask." He glanced toward the bank of the creek and saw that Jenny was still in view, even though she had her back to them for the moment.

He dropped his voice even lower. "I want very much to kiss you." He allowed the thought to linger between them, allowed the color to climb in her cheeks and the anticipation to shine in her eyes before adding, "But I won't. Not with Jenny so close by again."

It might have been his imagination or wishful thinking, but he thought he detected disappointment shadowing the depths of her eyes even as she murmured her thanks.

He grinned. "That doesn't mean I can't tell you what I think kissing you would be like. Your mouth is soft as a rose petal, Janet Runningbear, and your breath is just as sweet. I love the way your eyes darken when my mouth is this close to yours," he said, leaning down to within a hairbreadth of her lips, then retreating almost at once. This time he heard the shock of her indrawn breath and knew, absolutely knew, that what he saw in her eyes was disappointment.

He ran his thumb along her lower lip. "There will be other times," he assured her. "Private times."

He released her then, amused that she stood as if his hands were still on her, quiet and shaken. He hoped his own emotions weren't half so apparent. One thing for sure, he wasn't half as frightened of what the future might hold as she appeared to be. For the first time since they'd met, she seemed truly vulnerable.

For the life of him, he couldn't decide if that was good or bad. Until he could figure it out, he settled for taming the electricity arcing through the air so they could get through the rest of the day without giving Jenny something more to fret about.

He winked at her. "Come on, woman. Why are you standing there? We've got fried chicken and potato salad and coleslaw to serve up. You must be starving after that ride."

She visibly shook off the uncertainties that had held her still. "You're right. I am famished." She scanned the creek bank until she found Jenny, then called her, just a hint of desperation in her voice. "Come on, sweetie. Lunch is ready."

Harlan settled himself in his favorite position against the tree and listened to Janet and Jenny chatter through lunch. If there was a nervous edge to the conversation, he chalked it up to the electricity that his best effort had failed to diffuse. For better or worse, the attraction humming between Janet and him was powerful stuff. It needed only a chance look, a casual touch, to set it off.

"Is the creek deep enough to swim in?" Jenny asked after they'd eaten. "I wore my suit under my jeans."

"How'd you know about the creek and guess we'd be coming here?" Harlan asked, more amused than ever by her earlier grudging comparison of the creek to the ocean.

"Cody showed me," she said, shrugging, her expression all innocence. "He said it was your favorite place. When you invited Mom to go riding, I knew you'd end up here."

That explained the swimsuit and her earlier derisive reaction. The creek had probably looked much more interesting when she'd been here with Cody, Harlan decided. It also explained her determination to come along today. She hadn't wanted her mother alone with him in such a romantic setting.

"Can I go in the water, Mom?"

"Not right after lunch," Janet said at once.

"She'll be fine," Harlan said. "The creek's only waist high at its deepest."

Janet still seemed uneasy—about the swim or being left alone with him, it was hard to tell—but she gave permission.

"You could go in, too," Harlan said when Jenny had run off.

"I didn't wear my suit," she said.

"That's not a problem. Strip down over behind those trees. I won't peek. Cross my heart."

"Yeah, right," she said, amusement making her eyes sparkle.

Harlan's pulse bucked like a bronco. She looked ten years younger all of a sudden. That was the way of flirting, he decided. It lifted spirits and drained away problems, at least for a moment in time. It brought back that starry-eyed anticipation that regrettably seemed to fade once youth had passed by.

"If it's all the same to you, I'll stay right here, where it's safe," she said.

"Darlin', if you think it's safe here with me, your judgment has more problems than that old car of yours."

To his surprise, she grinned. "But you're an honorable man and you've already promised that absolutely nothing will happen as long as Jenny is around."

"That promise didn't allow for the temptation factor. You keep taunting me and I can't be responsible for my actions."

"Then by all means, let's change the subject. Tell me about White Pines."

He leaned back against the tree and linked his hands behind his head just to keep himself from reaching for her.

"It's been in my family since the time of the Civil War," he said, thinking back to all the history that Mary had loved so deeply. She'd been far more fascinated by the Adams legacy than he had been. He'd just loved the land and ranching. It was as deeply ingrained in his blood as whatever DNA there was to identify him.

"That's how it got its name," he continued. "My ancestors moved here from the South and called it White Pines, just like the plantation that had been burned to the ground by Yankee soldiers. Texas seemed like a land of opportunity back then, I suppose. They came here with very little, but with grit and determination the next generations added to that beginning until it became what you see today. The Mexican settlers in the area named the town Los Piños after the ranch, which provided work for so many of the families."

At some point as he talked, a change came over Janet's face. Suddenly she was more aloof than ever and a kind of seething resentment burned in her eyes.

"Is something wrong?" he asked, thoroughly bemused by the change in her.

"Not really," she said, and stood, brushing off her jeans.

The innocent gesture drew attention to her shapely rear end and had Harlan's blood sizzling like an adolescent boy's. But he was too puzzled by the abrupt change in her demeanor to enjoy his reaction for very long.

"Janet?"

"We'd better be getting back."

"You'll stay for supper," he said, making it more a matter-of-fact statement than a question.

She hesitated for just an instant, clearly wrestling with indecision, her expression uncertain, then shook her head. "No. That wouldn't be a good idea."

"Why?"

"It just wouldn't, that's all. We've taken up too much of your time as it is."

Harlan frowned. "What the devil is that supposed to mean?"

"Forget it," she muttered. With that, she bolted in the direction of where Jenny was swimming in the creek. "Jenny, come on now, sweetie. It's time to go."

Janet's strange mood lasted all the way back to the house. For the life of him, Harlan couldn't figure out what had gone wrong. One thing was certain, though. Janet was far more of a mystery than the woman who'd been his mate for more than thirty-five years.

She was strong, as Mary had been. But she was also fiercely independent, burned by what he could only guess had been a lousy childhood and an even lousier marriage. There were apparently other dark secrets he hadn't even begun to discover.

Whatever those secrets might be, he had the feeling her heart had turned to ice in the process. Knowing that might have discouraged some men, but not him. He had a hunch that melting it was going to be downright interesting.

Chapter Eight

No amount of persuading had been able to convince Janet and Jenny to stay for supper on Saturday or to return on Sunday. Harlan decided he must be losing his touch. He thought he'd tried some very inventive arguments, along with a little subtle flirting and a few dares. There had been a brief spark in Janet's eyes at one point, but she'd still managed to decline the invitation, albeit with a satisfyingly obvious hint of regret in her voice.

Watching them leave, he resigned himself to waiting impatiently for Monday morning when Janet would return to drop off Jenny. Maybe then Jenny would be able to shed some light on her mother's abrupt shift in mood.

In the meantime, the hours stretched out ahead of him, promising nothing but tedium. Now that he was starting to feel alive again, he was even less tolerant of the prospect than he had once been.

Short of booting Cody out of his position as ranch manager, he wasn't sure what to do about it. Los Piños was too small a town to need an influential citizen meddling in its affairs. State or national politics had never intrigued him. In fact, the only things that had ever mattered to him were his family and the ranch.

After church on Sunday, he spent most of the remainder of the morning wandering through all the empty rooms at White Pines, trying to remember the days when his sons had made the kind of racket that drove Mary nuts, trying to imagine the big old house echoing with laughter once again.

Jenny's presence lately had given him a delightful hint of what it might be like, at least when she let down her guard long enough to act like a regular thirteen-year-old. Occasionally she and some of Maritza's younger relations would whoop it up in the kitchen, usually when she counted on him being out of earshot. The joyous sound, when he happened to catch it, brightened his day.

Now, though, he tried to picture the generations before him, who had built the ranch into a thriving enterprise. He knew almost nothing about those early days beyond the scant information he'd shared with Janet. Mary had always been exasperated with him for caring so little about the past. He'd been more concerned with the future, with making White Pines into a legacy for his sons and their children.

Ironically, only Cody had really cared about his heritage. Ranching was in his blood, just as it had been in Harlan's. Luke had loved ranching well enough, but he'd had a milewide independent streak that pushed him into starting up his own place, not just as proof that he could succeed at it, but to best his father. Cody had the same goal, it seemed to him. He was just more willing to fight Harlan one-on-one, on his home turf. He seemed to thrive on the war of wills.

Jordan and Erik hadn't been interested in White Pines or ranching at all. In fact, it had been attempts to force Erik into a life that was never right for him that had ultimately led to his death. Riding a tractor one day at Luke's, he'd gotten careless. The tractor had rolled over on him and killed him, leaving Jessie a widow and expecting his child.

Ultimately, Luke had claimed both mother and child, a beautiful Christmas baby named Angela. As happy as they were, Harlan wondered sometimes if they'd ever forget the cost at which that happiness had come.

With Jordan in the oil business and living at the ranch that had belonged to his wife Kelly's family, now only Cody and Melissa and their kids remained at White Pines. Even they, however, lived in their own home, rather than in one of the suites that had been created to house new generations at a time when Harlan had imagined spending his golden years surrounded by family. They were close by, but not nearly close enough to keep him from rattling around in these lonely old rooms.

Only a few hours after his uncommon bout of self-pity, Harlan cursed himself for regretting the lack of company. It just proved that a man should be careful what he wished for.

Cody and Melissa arrived on his doorstep first with their kids, Sharon Lynn and Harlan Patrick. He could tell right off this was no drop-by visit for a quick hello. They seemed ready to settle down for a bit. They'd brought along enough paraphernalia for the kids to entertain them until nightfall.

Luke and Jessie were hard on their heels with precious, sweet-faced Angela. Jordan and Kelly turned up within minutes after that with Dani and Justin James. It was a conspiracy, no doubt about that. He didn't believe for a second they'd all shown up just to get a decent meal from Maritza.

Apparently his housekeeper had known they were coming, though. He noticed that she'd set places for every traitorous one of them at his table.

"So, Daddy, anything interesting going on around here?" Luke inquired after Maritza had served a prime rib big enough to feed an expected crowd, but far too big to pass off as something she'd prepared just for one. Not even his impudent housekeeper was brazen enough to suggest she was having to stretch the lavish spread of food to accommodate unexpected guests.

"Other than the lot of you showing up to beg a meal?" he retorted. "Not a thing."

"Have you met the new lawyer in town?" Jordan inquired with a perfectly straight face. "What's her name? Janet Runningbear? I've spotted her a couple of times myself. She's gorgeous. You thought so, too, didn't you, Cody?"

Harlan scowled at Cody and Melissa, who were looking about as innocent as a couple of tattletales could. If he'd had any doubts about his youngest son having the biggest mouth in the family, his proof was sitting around his dining room table right now.

It was obvious Luke and Jessie and Jordan and Kelly knew every last detail of his fledgling fascination with Janet Runningbear. They'd probably been told the second Cody had finished listening to all of his confessions about that night in Janet's kitchen. That poker game at Rosa's hadn't helped. What Cody hadn't blabbed himself, Rosa had.

"We've met," he admitted tersely, trying hard to avoid making the kind of revelations that would invite more taunting.

Cody chuckled, then covered his face with a napkin to hide his smile.

"Damn your hide, boy," Harlan said to his youngest. "You got any control whatsoever over that mouth of yours?"

"I can't imagine what you mean," Cody declared, feigning a hurt expression that was about as believable as the ones he'd worn on his chocolate-streaked face when he'd sworn he'd never been near the cookie jar.

"If anyone's to blame, it's you," Cody added, trying to pass on the guilt. "You're the one who made a spectacle of yourself at Rosa's. It was the hottest story on the Los Piños grapevine for a solid week. Mule filled in any gap Rosa left in the story. Seemed to enjoy it, too. All I did was confirm a few facts, when asked directly.''

''It was a poker game, not a spectacle,'' Harlan retorted defensively. ''Playing cards wasn't a crime last time I checked.''

''From what I heard, poker wasn't exactly the only game being played that afternoon,'' Jordan chimed in with a wicked grin.

Harlan resigned himself to sitting back and taking whatever they were of a mind to dish out. To his surprise, though, he found an unexpected ally in Jessie. She reached over and patted his hand.

''I think all of you should leave your father alone,'' she protested to the others, a twinkle in her blue eyes. ''He obviously doesn't require your meddling in order to have a social life.''

All three of his sons hooted. ''Meddling?'' Luke said to his wife. ''You call this meddling? This is child's play compared to what he put all of us through. You and me included, in case you've forgotten.''

''I still think you should leave him alone,'' Jessie repeated firmly.

''Thank you,'' Harlan said. ''But I think you're wasting your breath with this band of hooligans.''

''I still have a little influence with one of them,'' she said, shooting a pointed look at Luke, who was seated on her other side.

"Right," Jordan said. "And I suppose those bags you toted upstairs a little while ago don't indicate that you and Lucas intend to stay right here until morning, just so you can catch a glimpse of Janet Runningbear and her daughter. I'd be happy to describe her, if you'd like to turn right around and go back home. Tall, slender, mid-thirties, long black hair. Is that what you were wondering about?"

"It's a start," Luke confirmed.

This was definitely a turn of events Harlan hadn't counted on. Janet was skittish enough around him without having to face his whole darn family. He scowled at Luke. "You're staying?"

"Just till dawn," he said with a grin. "I'd hate to make that long drive back tonight. I might fall asleep at the wheel. Besides, you don't get to see nearly enough of Angela. She misses her granddaddy. Isn't that right, sweet pea?"

The toddler dutifully scrambled off her chair and ran around to be picked up so she could deliver sticky kisses to Harlan's face. "Miss you, grandda," she asserted enthusiastically.

"Did you coach her to do that, just so I wouldn't toss you out on your ear?" Harlan grumbled.

Jordan glanced across the table at his wife. "Maybe we should stick around, too. What do you think?"

"I think Luke is perfectly capable of tormenting your father without any help from you," Kelly retorted.

"Thank you," Harlan said to her.

"But I want to stay," Dani protested. The seven-year-old's expression turned wily. "I can help baby-sit Angela. Aunt Jessie says I'm really, really good."

"Oh, for goodness' sake, the whole darn lot of you might as well move back in," Harlan declared.

"Don't tempt us, Daddy," Luke advised. "We just might do it, at least until we see where things between you and Janet Runningbear are heading. By the way, have you been locking up all the cars now that her daughter's around here all the time?"

Harlan groaned. He'd always wanted a tight-knit family. He'd always done his darnedest to make his sons feel welcome at White Pines, even after they'd gone on to lives of their own. It appeared he was going to live to regret not booting them all into another state. For the second time in a little more than an hour, he reminded himself to be very, very careful what he wished for in the future.

Janet took one look at the assembled members of Harlan Adams's family as she drove up to the house on Monday and very nearly turned tail and ran. She didn't have a doubt in the world that she and Jenny were the main attraction that had drawn them onto the porch at daybreak. All of the family, she guessed from the size of the gathering, right down to the youngest grandchild. Even her intrepid daughter seemed a little awed by all the attention riveted on them.

"Who are all those people and why are they staring at us?" Jenny asked, regarding the bunch of them warily.

"Now you know how Custer must have felt when he made his last stand," Janet said dryly, then added, "My guess is they're all here to try to figure out if we have designs on their father."

"You mean like wanting to marry him or something?" Jenny asked, astonishment written all over her face.

"That would be my guess," Janet confirmed.

Jenny's mouth gaped. "You don't, do you?"

"I don't," Janet said emphatically.

She wished she could speak with as much certainty about Harlan's intentions. He was the first man in aeons who wasn't the least bit put off by her prickly, independent nature. Even after she'd turned moody on him on Saturday, he'd remained flirtatious and placid.

In fact, if anything, the glint in his eyes burned even brighter in the face of her contrariness. He wanted her and that, in his opinion, was that. He clearly thought it was just a matter of time until he got his way.

Apparently his sons thought as much, too, or they wouldn't be here this morning trying to check out the woman who'd caught their father's eye.

"Go on and hop out," she advised Jenny.

"You're going to leave me here alone with *them?*" her daughter protested, clearly aghast at the prospect. "I don't think so."

"Jenny, I'm sure they're all very nice people."

"Then why are you running away?"

"Because they obviously have an agenda I don't want to deal with," she said.

She cast a quick look to see if she could turn her car around in this unoccupied corner of the driveway or if she was going to be forced to circle all the way around in front of the house, in front of all those fascinated, prying eyes.

Jenny folded her arms over her chest and lifted her chin. Defiance radiated from every pore. "I am not getting out of this car without you."

"Sweetie, please," she implored.

"No way."

"You'll embarrass Harlan."

"And your taking off won't?" Jenny flung back. "Get real, Mom. They're here to check you out even more than me. Maybe you should prepare a little speech denying any interest in Mr. Adams. Maybe then they'd go away."

Janet sighed and threw the car into park and shut off the engine. "Traitor," she muttered at her daughter.

"Don't blame me. Blame Mr. Adams."

Janet glanced in Harlan's direction. He looked every bit as miserable as she felt. "I seriously doubt that this was his idea of a good time," she observed.

"Then he should have kicked them out," Jenny retorted. "If he can't control his own kids, how come you think he's such a good influence on me?"

"It's hardly the same," Janet replied.

"I don't see why. If I'm going to turn out all nosy like them, I'd think you'd want to get me away from here as fast as you could."

Before Janet could come up with an adequate answer for that, Harlan was opening her door.

"I'm sorry," he said in a hushed tone. "I didn't know they were coming yesterday and I sure as hell didn't know they were staying. I couldn't shake 'em out of here to save my soul. I thought about starving them out, but my housekeeper would have fed them behind my back, I'm sure."

His genuine discomfort relieved some of her own tension. "Jenny thinks you have a serious inability to control your own kids."

He grinned. "I couldn't have said it better myself. I'm still not sure where I went wrong." He held out his hand to her. "Come on. We might as well get this over with. Give it five minutes and you can swear you have a major client coming and that you have to get to town."

She suddenly found his desire to be rid of her in such a hurry a little insulting. "Are you afraid to let them spend too much time with me?" she asked irritably.

His mouth gaped. "With you? Are you crazy? I'm scared silly you'll take one look at the lot of them and never show your face around here again."

She grinned at his adamant tone. "I'm made of tougher stuff than that," she declared. "So is Jenny." She leaned back in. "Out, young lady."

Jenny rolled her eyes. "Oh, all right. But I'm not playing cute for anybody, okay?"

"There was little doubt of that," Janet said dryly, exchanging a pointed look with Harlan, who looked as if he wanted very badly to burst out laughing.

As they approached the porch, three young women came down the steps to meet them.

"Hi, I'm Jessie," the first one said. "We're sorry about all of this, but there's no controlling these guys when they get together to harass their father. We couldn't have gotten them out of here last night if we'd set off a canister of pepper spray in the house. Believe me, I thought about it. So did Kelly and Melissa."

"I even had one in my purse," Kelly said. "I bought it when I lived in Houston. Never had a need for it there, thank goodness, but I thought it might come in handy here last night."

"Too many babies, though," Melissa added. "I'm talking about the ones in cribs, not the ones we're married to. You'd think they hadn't learned to share, the way they've been carrying on about meeting the woman who's stealing their daddy's affection."

Janet warmed to the trio of smiling women immediately. They clearly understood what it meant to hook up with an Adams man. "Believe me, I am not out to steal their daddy's affection or anything else, for that matter."

"It's not entirely up to you," Jessie declared with the kind of clear-thinking logic that cut straight to the heart of Janet's dilemma. "Our husbands may be the stubbornnest set of men in Texas. Not a one of them knows how to take no for an answer. Who do you guess they learned that from?"

"Hey," Harlan protested. "Watch your tongue."

"It's true, Harlan, and you know it," Kelly and Melissa chimed in, laughing at his disgruntled expression.

Janet considered the teasing comments to be very discouraging news. Apparently Harlan detected her discomfort, because he slipped her arm through his.

"Come on," he said. "We might as well get the rest of this over with. Ladies, go tell your husbands to be on their best behavior."

"Don't expect us to accomplish what you couldn't," Kelly teased.

Jenny rolled her eyes. "I told you, Mom."

Harlan glanced at her. "What did you tell your mother?"

"That you must not be half so tough as you try to pretend, if your sons walk all over you."

The sons in question hooted at that.

"Guess she has you pegged, doesn't she, Daddy?" Cody taunted.

"If her mama's half as smart, you're in for it," Jordan agreed, grinning at Janet as he shook her hand.

Luke crowded in next, a sympathetic glimmer in his eyes. "Don't let all the fuss scare you to death. We're not half as intimidating as we sound."

"A bunch of soft touches?" Janet asked doubtfully.

He nodded. "And Daddy's the easiest of all."

"You start giving away all my secrets and that prize bull of mine you want to breed next year won't get anywhere near those cows of yours," Harlan warned.

Luke held up his hands and backed off. "Not another word," he vowed.

The teasing went on for another ten minutes, though, as the three oldest grandchildren raced around the yard. Jenny seemed thoroughly bemused by all the commotion. It made Janet wonder whether she'd been so wrong to insist to Barry that she wanted no more children. Left unspoken had been the fact that she didn't want them with him. Within months of Jenny's birth, she had already sensed that their marriage wasn't going to last the distance. It had taken her more than twelve years to finally cut the ties.

When Melissa shoved a baby into her arms, so she could chase after her daughter who was vanishing around the side of the house, Janet felt a stirring of maternal instinct that was so overwhelming it brought tears to her eyes. She quickly handed the baby over to Jessie, who was standing nearby.

"I have to get to work," she announced to no one in particular.

Harlan was at her side in a heartbeat. "We'll talk later," he said as he walked with her to her car. "I'll come up with some way to apologize for all this."

"It's not like you threw me into a den of starving wolves," she reminded him. "It wasn't that bad. They're nice people, all of them. And they clearly love you and worry about you."

He grinned at that. "Do I look like a man who needs people fussing over him?"

She couldn't help smiling at that. "I doubt they see you the same way I do," she said.

"Oh, really," he said, sounding absolutely fascinated all of a sudden. "And how do you see me?"

"Never mind. Your ego's big enough as it is," she said, and closed the car door in his face.

"We'll finish this discussion tonight," he shouted as she drove away.

The challenge in his voice and the gleam in his eyes stayed with her the rest of the day. At least a dozen times, as she talked with the few potential clients who called, an image of Harlan's face popped into her head. His strength and compassion, along with that taunting, unmistakable desire, kept her from regretting the day she'd moved to Texas.

Too many of the calls were from people only interested in hiring her if she'd work free, or from people with ugly accusations to make about her being an uppity Indian. She found the atmosphere of bias and distrust both discouraging and infuriating.

By the time she returned to White Pines to pick up Jenny, she had a thundering headache and a chip on her shoulder the size of a longhorn. The sight of Harlan waiting on the porch for her, a pitcher of tea ready, along with more of Maritza's culinary treats, brought tears to her eyes. She lingered in the car for a moment for fear he'd see how despondent she was and try to jump in and fix things for her. After a day like the one she'd just had, it would be too easy simply to let him.

Even though she'd taken the time to gather her composure, Harlan wasn't fooled. He took one look at her and reached out to gather her into his arms. She hesitated only an instant before accepting the comfort he offered.

"Bad day?" he asked.

"Is it that obvious?"

"To me, it is. Want to talk about it?"

She wrapped her arms a little tighter around his waist and rested her head on his chest. "No, but this is nice."

Too nice, she reminded herself sternly. Too easy. It was a dangerous trap. With a sigh, she pulled away. "Thanks."

"You could stay right where you are," he said. "These are mighty broad shoulders. Might as well make use of 'em, if you've got troubles."

"Nothing I can't handle," she said, and forced herself to step away from what he was offering.

When she would have turned away, his voice stopped her.

"Janet?" he said in little more than a whisper.

She lifted her gaze to his and felt her heart skip a beat at the blazing heat in his eyes. She swallowed hard. "Yes?"

"Jenny's off with Cody again. They're going to be a while. Care to take a chance on another kiss?"

She almost wished he hadn't asked at all, that he'd just swept her back into his arms without giving her any say in the matter. But she couldn't deny that a part of her was glad he'd reassured her of Jenny's whereabouts first.

"I can't," she protested halfheartedly, even as she swayed toward him.

He stroked a finger along her cheek. "Talk about mixed messages, darlin'."

She shook her head ruefully. "I know. I'm pitiful."

"Never pitiful," he argued. "Strong, sassy, impossible, maybe, but never pitiful."

His touch on her face lingered. There were a hundred questions in his eyes, but only one that really mattered: had she meant yes or no? Both, depending on whether he asked her head or her heart, she decided.

And just this once she was going with her heart. She stood on tiptoe to lift her lips to his. Her touch was tentative, but it was all it took to set passion blazing. So much tenderness. So much heat, she thought as he held her head still and plundered her mouth.

The rightness of it stunned her. He was everything she'd once been taught to hate by Lone Wolf—a Texan and a rancher. And yet, in his arms, as she was right now, she felt at home. At peace.

At least that was how she felt deep in her heart. Her head was another matter entirely. She had a hunch that struggle was far from over.

Chapter Nine

"Hot," Janet murmured eventually, backing away from Harlan as if he were a stove and she'd been standing over it too long. If she'd owned a hankie and it wouldn't have been a dead giveaway of how affected she was by his touch, she would have patted her brow with it.

"I'll say," he agreed, his eyes twinkling with amusement.

"I was referring to the temperature," she insisted as embarrassment made her face flush even hotter. At this rate she'd wind up as a little puddle of mortified genes right at his feet.

"Of course you were," he said perfectly innocently. "So was I."

"The weather, dammit!"

He nodded. "If you say so."

She turned her back on him and headed across the porch, trying not to mutter out loud about his impudence. On the way, she grabbed a glass of iced tea and held it against her feverish brow.

This attraction was getting out of hand. She was slipping into a pattern that had all the earmarks of surrender. It would be just her luck that she'd fall head-over-heels in love with Harlan Adams and then he'd discover that she was out to find a way to reclaim some of his land for the Comanches. He'd blow a gasket, blow her off, and they'd both wind up being hurt and feeling used.

She heard his booted footsteps as he crossed the porch to join her. He was moving slowly, almost as if he wanted to give her time to prepare. By the time he paused beside her, her nerves were jittery all over again. Damn, why did it have to be this particular man who made her feel like a whole, vibrant, sexy woman again?

"You still wrestling with yourself?" he inquired in that lazy tone that raised goose bumps up and down her spine.

"Wrestling, hell," she admitted. "It's all-out war."

He chuckled at that. "Good."

"You don't have to sound so complacent about it."

"Sure I do. That's the nature of an Adams man."

Despite herself, she laughed and shifted until she could look into his eyes. "Big egos, huh?"

"I prefer to think of it as self-confidence."

"You would. Arrogance by any other name is still a flaw, Harlan."

"I'm entitled to one serious defect, don't you think?"

She held back another urge to laugh. "Just one? That's all you're admitting to?"

"I'm not a fool, darlin'. I'm not admitting to a single one you haven't already discovered. You're searching so hard for more, I'd hate to spoil your fun."

"How altruistic," she retorted sourly, wondering when she'd become so transparent. Or was it just that Harlan had an innate knack for reading her, a knack that stemmed from fascination and concentration? Few men had ever studied her quite so intently, that's for sure. Barry had never even scratched the surface of her emotions. She couldn't decide whether to feel flattered or cornered that Harlan could.

He settled himself onto the porch railing, then pulled her between his thighs. She didn't even have the strength of will to resist.

The provocative position, the glitter of desire in his eyes, sent shivers of pure longing dancing through her. As dangerous as the reaction was, she couldn't have pulled back if her life depended on it.

He kept his hands loosely settled on her hips as if to convey she was free to go, if she chose...if she could.

"Your skin turns to fire when you're close to me like this," he observed.

"How polite of you to point it out," she said, but without nearly as much venom as she should have mustered. Besides, it was true. That was what had forced her away from him only moments before.

"Why does that bother you so much?" he asked. "Men and women have been attracted to each other from the beginning of time. It's natural."

"Sometimes the attraction's to the wrong person."

"You think I'm wrong for you?"

She nodded. "And I'm just as wrong for you."

"Why?"

She sighed, unwilling to spell it all out for him. "It's complicated. You'll just have to take my word for it."

Drawing in a deep breath, she leveled a serious look straight into his blue eyes. "If you can't, I'll have to stop coming around. I'll keep Jenny away, too. We'll find another way to pay for the repairs to your truck. I'll work it out with Mule."

"Your debt's not with Mule. It's with me," he insisted stubbornly.

"He's making the repairs, isn't he?"

"Forget the blasted bill," he said, his exasperation apparent in his tone. He lifted her aside and stood. "Your daughter stole my truck. I didn't call the sheriff because you agreed to let her work off the debt out here."

She stiffened at the reminder. "I wonder how the sheriff would feel about your taking the law into your own hands, devising your own brand of justice?"

He scowled at her. "You want to test him and find out?"

Janet had a feeling that—laws or no laws—he knew the justice system in Los Piños and could manipulate it far better than she ever could with her legal expertise and law school degree.

"Why are you making this so difficult?" she snapped. "Hasn't anyone ever turned you down before?"

A ghost of a smile played around his lips. "Haven't asked anyone until you came along, not for more than thirty-five years."

That sucked the wind right out of her sails. She reached up impulsively and placed her hand against his cheek. "Harlan Adams, you don't play fair."

"That's right, darlin'. I play to win."

Before she could reply to that, his mouth was moving over hers again, coaxing, persuading, claiming.

It was a hell of a kiss by anyone's standards. By Janet's, it was devastating. A bone-melting, breath-stealing crack of thunder deep inside her. It raised goose bumps from head to toe and had the hair on the back of her neck raised on end.

"I think I'd better be going," she murmured when it was over. As badly as she wanted to sound serene and unfazed, she couldn't seem to get her voice above a shaken whisper. She glanced around anxiously, trying to spot the purse she'd dropped somewhere.

"Without Jenny?" he inquired, laughter dancing in his eyes.

"Oh," she murmured. "No, of course not." She drew in a deep, supposedly calming breath. It didn't help a whit.

"How soon will she and Cody be back?" she asked a little desperately.

"Not for a while," he reported complacently. "You might as well settle back and relax."

Relax? It would take an entire bottle of tranquilizers to get her to relax as long as Harlan was in the vicinity. She didn't have so much as a single pill to her name. She sipped at the only available distraction, her iced tea, but it didn't go far in terms of settling her nerves or soothing the thirst that kiss had aroused.

"You look as if you could use a nice, cool shower," Harlan said after a bit.

Her head snapped up. "What?"

"A cool shower," he prompted, grinning. "Alone, if that's the way you prefer."

"Here?" she asked incredulously.

"Why not? It's a big house. There are lots of bathrooms. If I'd put in that pool the boys were always plaguing me to, I'd suggest that, but a shower is all I have to offer."

The offer might have been part generosity, part seduction, but Janet was intrigued just the same. Maybe an ice-cold shower would get her through the wait, she decided thoughtfully. It would wash away some of the hot day's dust and cleanse her wicked thoughts at the same time.

And maybe not. She weighed just how far she could trust Harlan to stay right here where he was, rather than following her inside.

Don't be an idiot, she lectured herself. Of course, he would stay here. The man was a gentleman... when it suited his purposes.

As if he'd read the temptation in her eyes, he said, "Use the bathroom in Luke's suite. It's the first one upstairs on the right. I think Jessie probably left some of that fancy, perfumed bubble bath she likes, if you'd prefer to relax in a tub for a while.''

The suggestion conjured up images so steamy her brain should have been x-rated. ''A shower will be fine,'' she said, bolting to presumed safety.

Inside Luke's suite, with the door locked, and inside the bathroom with *that* door locked, she leaned back against it and released a pent-up breath. Safe at last, she thought. What was yet to be determined, however, was whether she was hiding from Harlan's pursuit or her own increasingly dangerous longings.

Damn, but she was a stubborn one, Harlan thought to himself the following morning as he surveyed the disaster Jenny had made of his toolshed. Almost as stubborn as her mama.

Janet's abrupt retreat to hide out in Luke's suite until Jenny's return the night before had left him chuckling on the front porch. Frustrated as hell, but amused just the same. There'd been no mistaking how grateful Janet had been to be given a reason to escape his provocative company for a bit.

Jenny had shown up finally, looking for her mama. When Harlan had told her she was inside taking a bath, Jenny's shocked expression suggested she was making far more of that than she should have. Thank goodness Cody wasn't with her or he'd have had a few choice words to add to the conversation for sure.

Harlan had instantly regretted any inferences Jenny might have made, but he hadn't been able to think of any way to correct her mistaken impression without adding to the problem.

"Tell her I'm waiting in the car," she'd said stiffly, and stalked away, her back as straight and proud as any Comanche chief he'd ever seen pictured in the art museums around the Southwest.

"Sure you don't want a glass of tea or maybe some of the oatmeal-and-raisin cookies Maritza baked earlier?" he'd called after her. He'd seen his plans for an evening with the two of them vanishing in a puff of smoke. Janet was scared spitless of being around him and Jenny clearly resented whatever was happening between him and her mother.

The offer of cookies went unanswered, just one indication of how upset she'd been. When he'd relayed her whereabouts to her much cooler-looking, if no less rattled mother, Janet had grabbed her purse and taken off without so much as a goodbye.

"Well, that certainly went well," he'd muttered as he'd watched the trail of dust settle in their wake.

Apparently their evening hadn't gotten any better, if Jenny's sullen mood this morning was any indication. She wouldn't even meet his gaze, which made him wonder just what Janet had told her about their little set-to the night before.

At midmorning, as soon as she'd picked disinterestedly at the snack Maritza had prepared for her, she'd stalked out of the kitchen and disappeared, sparing him little more than a glare.

He hadn't seen her for another hour or so. Hadn't even looked that hard, truthfully. He'd figured she needed time to settle down and get her bearings again without him hovering over her with a lot of questions.

Then, not more than five minutes ago, he'd spotted her sneaking away from the toolshed with suspicious streaks of yellow paint on her clothes. It was not a good sign, he'd decided as he went out to the shed.

The shambles he found triggered an explosion that could have been heard in the next county. Toolboxes had been upended, yellow paint had been splattered hither and yon, and nuts, bolts and nails were scattered like birdseed all over the floor.

"Damn that girl's hide!" he bellowed, even as he wondered precisely what had set her off this time. He'd long since discovered that Jenny only acted out when she was feeling threatened in some way.

Taking off in the direction he'd seen her heading, he followed her trail all the way to the creek. He found her sitting at the edge, her feet in the water, tears streaming down her face.

He lowered himself to the ground next to her and waited, biding his time until she felt like talking.

"I don't care if you do send me to jail," she said eventually in a voice choked with barely contained sobs.

"Actually, I hadn't considered that possibility," he said. "I was thinking you could spend the rest of the day back there cleaning up the mess you made."

He looked her in the eye and saw thirteen years of hurt and loneliness there. "First, though, why don't you tell me what's on your mind?"

"Nothing."

"You just decided to tear up things inside the toolshed for fun?"

"So what if I did?" she said belligerently.

"I suppose everybody gets in a foul mood on occasion for no reason and needs to let off a little steam," he agreed, then slanted a look at her. "Just seems to me as if something must have set you off."

"Well, it didn't, all right!"

He shrugged. "If you say so."

For the next few minutes they sat there side-by-side in total silence except for the sound of birds singing in the trees overhead and the soft splash of the creek as it ran past.

"You just gonna drop it?" she asked, regarding him with a mix of surprise and wariness.

"I thought there was nothing you wanted to say. Of course, maybe if you tell me, you'll feel better. That's how it works sometimes. Sharing the load goes a long way toward making it seem a little lighter."

Her shoulders slumped dejectedly as she picked at the frayed edge of her cut-off jeans. "You'll get mad."

"So it has something to do with me?"

She nodded, looking miserable.

"Is it me and your mom?"

Her head gave an almost imperceptible little bob. "I think she likes you," she mumbled finally. "She says she doesn't, but I can tell."

Harlan considered the observation a promising sign. He didn't tell Jenny that. She obviously disagreed.

"Would that be so terrible, having your mom like me?" he asked instead, hoping to get to the root of her displeasure. Did she resent the possibility of a replacement for her father? Was it just him in particular she disliked? He had a feeling the answer might hold the key to his future.

"It's not that exactly," she admitted. "I mean, you're okay, I guess. A little bossy, but okay. It's just that my mom and me, we've been a team ever since the divorce. We don't need anybody else."

"Maybe I do," he said quietly.

The concept seemed to intrigue her. "What do you mean?"

"Just that it's been awful quiet around here the past year or so, ever since my wife died. My sons are all grown and living their own lives now."

"Maybe Cody and his kids could move in with you," she suggested, either in an attempt to be helpful or an attempt to get her and her mother off the hook.

He could have given some glib reply to that, but he decided she needed honesty from him. She needed to be treated like an adult, at least on this issue. "Oh, the truth of it is, Cody and I would butt heads constantly. And Melissa should be able to run her own house the way she wants without worrying about the way things were always done around here."

She nodded thoughtfully. "That could be a problem, I guess. So how come you like having me and my mom around so much?"

"For one thing, you're a pretty special kid, in case you didn't know. I knew it the second you climbed down out of that truck of mine, spitting mad and taking your own foolishness out on me.''

He slanted a sideways look at her. She appeared to be listening intently, so he went on. ''As for your mom, she's made me laugh again. That's mighty important. It's always seemed to me that folks weren't meant to go through life without a companion, someone who thinks they're terrific. I don't know a lot about what happened between your parents, but divorce is never easy. I think you and your mom deserve someone who'll put your needs first. And I could sure use someone to liven this place up.''

Jenny looked torn between wanting him to feel better and her own distinctly opposite needs. ''Maybe you could just play the radio real loud or 'Geraldo' and 'Oprah.' Wouldn't that work?''

He grinned. ''It's not the same.''

''You mean you just want people to talk to, stuff like that?''

''More or less.''

''Oh.'' She seemed to be considering the idea, then she lifted her chin and stared him straight in the eye. ''I thought you wanted sex with her.''

The blunt and far too perceptive remark sent blood climbing up the back of his neck. He had to choke back a chuckle. ''That's a whole other issue and one I do not intend to discuss with you, young lady,'' he said sternly.

''My mother and I talk about everything. She doesn't keep secrets,'' she said, regarding him with a sly look. ''Not from me, anyway.''

"I'll bet she'll keep this one," Harlan countered. It was beginning to seem to him, though, that there were too damned many people fascinated with his love life these days.

"So?" he asked. "What's the verdict? Do you object to your mom and me seeing each other?"

"Would you stop if I did?"

"Probably not," he admitted. "But I'd work like crazy to make you change your mind."

"Would you let me off this prison sentence you imposed?"

He grinned at the ploy. "Is being out here really so terrible?" He fixed a steady gaze on her. "Tell the truth."

"No," she said with an air of resignation. "It's just the principle of it. You get to boss me around and I have to take it."

"That's right," he said. "That's the way it works in the real world."

"Yeah, but in the real world you get paid. I'm doing slave labor."

He nodded. "Okay, maybe I didn't set up the rules quite right. How about we go back to the house and figure out how much you owe me for the truck—and the toolshed," he added pointedly. "Then we'll set a salary for your chores around here. You can pay me back out of your earnings each week."

"Will I have to pay you every dime?"

He chuckled at her negotiating skills. He'd raised one son who'd had the same knack for getting his way. He was head of an oil company now. He suspected Jenny could share a similar fate if she put that quick thinking of hers to good use.

"We can negotiate that," he suggested. "We'll work out an appropriate payment schedule. Of course, that might mean you won't be paid off at the end of summer. You might have to keep coming out here."

She weighed that for several minutes before nodding. "Okay."

He held out his hand. "Shall we shake on it?"

The instant they had solemnly shaken hands on their new deal, Jenny stood and whooped with undisguised glee. "I know exactly how I'm going to spend my money, too," she declared.

"How?" he said, anticipating a litany of CD titles and video games.

"I'm going to buy back Lone Wolf's land and give it to Mom."

He thought the plan might be a bit overly ambitious, given her debt and her likely wages, but who was he to discourage her. "And where is Lone Wolf's land?"

She grinned at him. "You're sitting on it."

Chapter Ten

This had been her great-great-grandfather's land? Harlan couldn't have been more stunned if Jenny had announced she and her mother had robbed a bank. He gazed around at the lush, verdant banks of the creek and beyond to the rolling landscape he'd always considered his home.

"You sure about that?" he asked, trying to piece together all of the implications. Was that why Jenny had stolen his truck in the first place, just to wrangle a meeting with him? Or maybe in some twisted way to get even with him for the perceived theft of her ancestor's land? It was certainly one explanation for the resentful expression he'd caught on Janet's face the day they'd gone riding over the ranch's acres.

It was several minutes before he realized Jenny hadn't answered. When he looked at her, he saw that she was scuffing the toe of her sneaker in the grass and looking guilty as sin. Since things like theft and destruction didn't stir that expression, he couldn't help wondering what had.

"Jenny?" he prodded. "How do you know that this was your great-great-grandfather's land?"

"Mom told me," she admitted, reluctance written all over her face. "I wasn't supposed to say anything, though. Please, don't say I told. Please."

There could only be one reason for keeping such a secret that he could think of. Janet had some cocka-mamie plan to right an old wrong and get this land back. He'd heard of court battles like that, efforts to reclaim Native American lands stolen by individuals or the government.

He didn't know of too many that had been successful, though. The government's treatment of Native American rights might have been shabby, but there were probably legal documents a foot thick to prove that the Native Americans had been compensated for every bit of land taken from them.

The thought that Janet might try, though, was enough to make his blood run cold. The knowledge that she had insinuated herself into his life without ever saying a word about her intentions infuriated him. He would have sworn Janet Runningbear didn't have a duplicitous bone in her body. It appeared his judgment had been impaired after all.

"Don't worry," he reassured Jenny with icy calm. "I won't say a thing to your mother."

No, he was going to sit back and wait for her to make her move. He would be ready for her, though. And he would make her regret the day she ever tried to tangle with Harlan Adams.

Later that night, alone in his den, he fought against the wave of disappointment rushing over him. He'd been so hopeful that Janet and her rebellious daughter were the answers to his prayers. Now it appeared that Janet, at least, was nothing more than a liar and a cheat.

He didn't like the prospect of sitting idle, waiting for her to strike. That wasn't his way.

And maybe he couldn't admit to all he knew and involve Jenny, but he could try to force Janet's hand. Maybe it was time he found out once and for all if it was him she was attracted to, or, as he was beginning to believe, the land she thought belonged to her.

With cold deliberation, he sat behind the desk where he'd kept White Pines books for so many years and plotted a strategy for making sure that not one single acre ever left Adams ownership. Janet Runningbear might be the smartest, slickest lawyer ever trained, but she was no match for him.

Except maybe, he thought, in bed. As icily furious as he was about Jenny's innocent revelations, he couldn't seem to tame the desire Janet aroused in him. Maybe sex was the way to force the issue. He could satisfy this growing hunger that had him aching to touch her morning, noon and night. A woman revealed a lot when she made love to a man. He was almost certain he would know once and for all what was really in Janet's heart, if he could just get past her emotional defenses.

He sipped on a glass of bourbon, pleased with his plan. His pulse kicked up just thinking about it. There was nothing like the prospect for steamy sex or a good battle of wills to make a man feel alive. He had Janet to thank on both counts, he thought with a trace of bitterness. He'd have to be sure to express his gratitude when all was said and done.

Janet glanced up with surprise when the door to her office opened at midmorning and Harlan stepped across the threshold onto the threadbare carpet she couldn't afford to replace until business picked up. Something in his expression alarmed her. She'd seen him looking determined. She'd seen him defiant. Both traits were evident now, but there was a cold, calculating gleam in his eyes that was something new and not entirely reassuring.

"What brings you into town?" she asked warily.

"I thought maybe you and I could get a word alone here."

She hadn't noticed that he had all that much difficulty getting her alone at White Pines when he was of a mind to, but she just nodded. "Something important come up?"

"In a manner of speaking," he said, perching on a corner of her desk, his jeans-clad knees scant inches from hers.

It seemed to Janet that he was deliberately crowding her. In fact, it was just more evidence of his odd mood. He had been acting weird all day. She'd noticed it first when she'd dropped off Jenny.

Now that she thought about it, Jenny had seemed awfully subdued since yesterday evening, as well. Had she gotten into more trouble? Was Harlan fed up with playing surrogate daddy? Had he come to tell her that he wanted to end their arrangement?

"Jenny's not giving you trouble, is she?" she asked, regarding him uneasily. Jenny, for all of her grumbling, would be heartbroken if her days at White Pines and with Harlan were over.

"None that I can't handle," he said.

The response relieved her mind on that score at least, but there was something. She was sure of it. "Then, what is it?" she prodded.

His gaze locked with hers. "I think we should go away together," he announced.

Oh, boy, she thought as the breath whooshed right out of her. This was the last thing she'd expected. Well, not the last thing, but certainly she hadn't anticipated such an invitation coming so soon. Janet felt her cheeks flame as she battled temptation and embarrassment.

"Go away together?" she repeated dazedly. "You and me? Why? I mean, we haven't even had a real date. Don't you think we're getting a little ahead of ourselves here?"

"We had dinner at your place. We've had dinner at my place. We've been on a picnic down by the creek. You don't call that dating?"

"No," she insisted. She didn't have a better name for it, but she'd been swearing to herself for days now that she was not dating Harlan Adams and that's the way she intended to keep it. "Even if those meals counted as dates, that's hardly a sufficient basis for assuming I would go off on some romantic tryst with you."

"I figured those kisses were a clue that you might at least consider the offer."

"Then you leapt to a wrong conclusion," she said adamantly.

An expression of pure frustration crossed his face. "Your daughter is asking me if I'm interested in having sex with you. My sons are practically salivating over every development in our relationship. I'd just like to get to know you someplace out from under their watchful eyes."

She stared at him with growing horror. "Jenny asked you about sex?" she asked with a sinking sensation in the pit of her stomach.

"Indeed she did," he said. "Not the workings of it, of course. Just whether that was the only reason I was interested in you."

"Oh, sweet heaven," she murmured. "I'm sorry."

He didn't seem to care about an apology. In fact, he seemed torn between exasperation and admiration for her child's audacity. She'd noticed that about him. Almost nothing threw Harlan Adams off stride. He was confident in a way that didn't require controlling other people. For all of the teasing she'd witnessed between him and his sons about his manipulation, she noticed that each of them had gone their own way, apparently with their father's blessing.

"I can't go away with you," she finally said with some regret. "I won't leave Jenny, for one thing. For another, I can't afford the damage to my reputation. I'm having enough difficulty getting the people in town to trust a woman lawyer, who's part Comanche, to boot, without giving them anything more to speculate about."

Harlan's expression promptly clouded over. "Are people still giving you a hard time? I thought that would be a thing of the past by now."

"It's no worse than I expected," she repeated emphatically, regretting taking that particular tack with him again. She knew better than to get his white knight tendencies stirred up.

"Who's bothering you?" he demanded, ignoring her low-key attempt to sidetrack him. "I'll have a word with them."

"No. You will not! We've been all through this. I will not have you fighting my battles for me. We're talking about my career. I can handle it."

He seemed ready and eager to rush off and slay a few dragons for her, but he finally backed down at her adamant tone. It was another thing she liked about him. He didn't just listen to her. He actually *heard* what she was saying.

Somewhere in a corner of her heart she was beginning to recognize that Harlan Adams wasn't like any other man she'd ever known. And all of those sturdy defenses that had served her so well the past few years were slowly but surely beginning to topple.

"Let's talk a little more about you and me, then," he suggested, shifting gears so quickly it left her head reeling. "Where do you see us heading?"

Janet wished she had prepared herself better for this moment. She had known a conversation like this was inevitable. Harlan wasn't the kind of man to be satisfied for long by evasive answers and rushed, skittish departures. She had no idea what had triggered this particular confrontation at midmorning in her office, rather than some evening out at White Pines, but apparently he'd reached a decision about the future and intended to put his plan into motion.

"I don't know where we're heading," she said, which was too close to the truth to suit her and too wishy-washy an answer to suit Harlan.

"You ever think about marrying again?" he asked.

She swallowed hard. "You mean, getting married to you?"

His gaze was riveted on her. "Or anyone," he conceded grudgingly.

Her throat went dry. She couldn't have croaked out a reply if she'd had one handy.

"Something wrong?" he inquired. "Cat got your tongue?"

An odd note in his voice triggered an alarm somewhere deep inside her. "Is there some reason you're forcing this issue now?"

"I just thought it was time to get our cards on the table." He studied her pointedly, then added, "All of our cards. Call the bet, so to speak."

Panic flooded through her. What exactly did he know? Had he somehow figured out her intentions about the Comanche lands? She'd been doing legal research in all her spare time, but no one knew about that, she reassured herself.

No one, except Jenny. Surely her daughter wouldn't have said a word. She knew how important silence was, especially when there was every chance in the world that nothing would come of her plans.

She studied Harlan's face and tried to guess what was going on behind that enigmatic expression. She had a feeling whatever decision she reached about that was critical. If she jumped to the wrong conclusion, said the wrong thing, it could ruin everything.

"My life's an open book," she said in what she hoped was an innocent-enough tone.

"Is it really?" he said, then shrugged. "I wasn't thinking so much of the past. I'm more concerned with the future."

"Harlan, I'm just a single mom struggling from day to day to make ends meet."

The comment sounded a little ingenuous even to her own ears. Harlan responded with a lift of his eyebrows, indicating that he wasn't fooled by it, either. Janet sighed.

"Okay, what do you want me to say?"

"How about the truth?" he said with a surprising edge in his voice. "Start to finish."

The last suggested for the second time in a matter of minutes that he knew something, or thought he did. "Harlan, is there something specific on your mind?"

"I've told you what was on my mind. It's your head that remains a mystery." He stood. "Why don't we go grab lunch and see if we can clarify a few things over a cold beer and some of Rosa's enchiladas?''

''The last time you and I went to Rosa's, I got the impression people were hanging on our every word and reporting it afterward. Why would you want to go there now?''

He shrugged. ''I was hoping the beer would loosen your tongue.''

She stared at him in exasperation. ''I'm being as honest here as I can be,'' she protested.

''Darlin', if this is your idea of being candid, I'd trust you to keep my deepest, darkest secrets.'' He stepped behind her and pulled back her chair. ''Come on. Let's see if a beer will work any magic or not.''

''I hate beer.''

''Then you'll drink it down right quick, sort of like medicine,'' he said, a glint of amusement in his eyes for the first time since he'd entered her office.

Janet still couldn't help thinking there were undercurrents here, deep ones, that she might never figure out. Something told her, though, that her future might depend on her trying.

A half dozen heads snapped up when Harlan escorted Janet through the door at Rosa's. Mule rolled his eyes in disgust.

''You two hooked up together again? Don't expect me to get involved in another poker game with the likes of you,'' the mechanic warned, scowling at Janet.

''Don't worry,'' Harlan informed him. ''We're here for a little private conversation.''

He passed right by his regular table and urged Janet into a booth all the way in the back. It wasn't quite out of the sight of prying eyes, but it was the best he could come up with under the circumstances.

"That was a little rude, don't you think?" Janet said when they were seated, a half dozen pairs of eyes staring at them. "Just the kind of thing that will stir up more gossip."

"Oh, will you stop fussing about gossip? Seems to me you have more important things to be fretting about."

"Such as?"

He reached across the table and touched a finger to her lower lip, all the while keeping his gaze locked with hers. "Such as the way your skin burns when I touch you like this."

He could feel her trembling even as she blinked hard and deliberately looked away. So, that much was real, he decided. She couldn't be faking a reaction like that, for devious purposes or otherwise. Which meant her reluctance to commit to anything more than the casual encounters they'd shared thus far was pure cussedness on her part.

Or perhaps a belated attack of ethical considerations, he amended. Maybe she'd decided she couldn't get any more involved with a man she intended to try to fleece out of his land. He supposed even would-be thieves had a code of honor they wouldn't breech.

He finally allowed his hand to drop away. "You trying to tell me that doesn't mean anything?" he chided.

"It doesn't," she insisted stubbornly.

"I don't believe you."

"Okay, I'm attracted to you," she snapped. "Is that what you wanted to hear? Does it make your heart go pitty-pat? Is your oversize ego satisfied?"

He chuckled at her irritation. "As a matter of fact, yes on all counts."

She lifted the menu and pointedly retreated behind it.

"You two planning on arguing all afternoon or were you thinking of ordering lunch?" Rosa inquired, not even trying to hide her amusement.

Harlan wondered with a sigh exactly how much she'd heard before she spoke up. He supposed whatever it was, his sons would know every word before nightfall. He wondered idly if Rosa's silence could be bought. He glanced up and studied her speculatively.

"Rosa, darlin', what would it take to keep you from telling Maritza or any of your other myriad relatives in Los Piños that I was even in here today?" he asked.

Janet peeked around her menu, curiosity written all over her face. "You're trying to bribe Rosa to keep silent?" she demanded.

"You bet," he muttered grimly. "Come on, Rosa, what will it take?"

The heavy-set Mexican woman shook her head as she regarded him with an expression of pity. "You cannot buy loyalty, old friend."

"I can't seem to get it, either," he grumbled. "Whatever you heard here today, just forget it, okay? That's not so much to ask, is it?"

Rosa's expression was perfectly bland. "But I heard nothing."

Harlan sighed. "I'll bet."

Not trusting her one whit, he still dropped the subject and asked Janet what she wanted. When he'd placed the order, he leaned back and focused once more on the woman seated opposite him.

The color in her cheeks was high. That was probably a sign of guilt, he decided. She'd wound her hair into some sort of prim knot on top of her head, but she'd done it in a way that made a man's fingers just itch to tug it free. He considered it another contradictory message in a whole sea of them he'd been getting lately.

As irritated and suspicious as he was, he wanted her with a hunger that stunned him. He'd been comfortable in his marriage with Mary. He'd enjoyed the physical side of their relationship. There'd still been plenty of passion to it. More than a lot of people shared after being together more than thirty-five years, from what he'd heard.

But these feelings he was experiencing now were a far cry from that. His pulse quickened just at the prospect of seeing Janet. His body responded like some randy adolescent's at the most innocent touch. A kiss was enough to trigger a desire so thorough and overwhelming, it was a wonder he hadn't busted the zipper of every pair of jeans he owned.

None of those reactions had eased just because he now suspected her of trying to cheat him out of his ranch. Was that because on some level he couldn't believe that's what she meant to do? Was he thinking with his testosterone and not his head? He wouldn't be the first man to fall prey to that sort of foolishness.

He met her gaze and tried to read her intentions in her dark brown eyes, but in the restaurant's shadows they were more inscrutable than ever.

"Harlan, what's really bothering you?" she asked, sounding more worried about him than frightened for herself. She didn't sound like a woman with secrets she feared might have been uncovered.

"I told you, I'm trying to get a grasp on what the future holds," he said, making the response enigmatic enough to cover anything from their relationship to the future of White Pines.

"Is that something you need to figure out today?" she asked, amusement lurking in her eyes. "Couldn't you just take it day by day as it comes, the way most of us mortals do?"

"I've never much liked surprises," he admitted.

"So it's true, then," she teased. "You do like to control everyone and everything around you. Your sons and daughters-in-law were right about that."

The truth chafed, especially when it was being used to suit the purposes of someone who didn't want to reveal her own intentions. "What's wrong with wanting to shape your life, with wanting to take charge and make it the best it can be?"

"You miss out on the serendipities," she observed.

"Like Jenny stealing my pickup, I suppose."

She grinned. "It's true. If you didn't make it a habit to leave your keys in plain view, that wouldn't have happened. Maybe you're more open to risks than you know."

"I don't mind a few risks, when I've had time to weigh the odds," he countered pointedly. "For forty years those keys had never been a temptation to anyone in Los Piños. Now those are odds worth taking a risk on."

He looked her straight in the eye. "You seem like a good risk to me, too."

She didn't seem pleased by the observation. "You make me sound like a filly you might bet on in the fifth race at Belmont."

He waved off the comparison. "That's just money. I'm talking about fate here, Janet. Yours and mine. You've been talking a lot about my willingness to take risks. What about you? How do you feel about serendipity?"

He watched her closely as she seemed to struggle with the question. Whatever internal war she was waging struck him as a pretty good indication that she did have things to hide.

"I'm all for it," she said eventually.

"Oh, really? Then why aren't you seizing my offer to take you away to some romantic spot for a few days?"

She scowled at him. "I explained that."

"Not to my satisfaction."

She stood then and threw down her napkin. "Not everything in this world has to meet your satisfaction, Harlan Adams. You'd do well to remember that."

With that she turned and sashayed straight out of Rosa's, ignoring the gaping expressions of Mule and all the others following her departure. To his ever-lasting regret, Harlan's body turned rock-hard just watching her go.

When she was finally out of sight, he sighed. That woman's defiant streak was going to be the death of him yet. Worse, he didn't know a damn bit more about what was going on in her head now than he had before he'd forced this confrontation. Yep, it was just as he'd suspected. He was definitely losing his touch.

Chapter Eleven

"Mom, did Mr. Adams seem weird to you to-day?" Jenny asked as she watched the hamburgers she had frying on the stove for dinner.

"Weird, how?" Janet replied, even though she thought she knew exactly what Jenny was talking about. He'd struck her as weird, impossible, arrogant and a whole lot more. She was interested, though, in just which vibes Jenny had picked up on.

"Like he was mad or something. I don't know. He was just awful quiet, not bossy like he usually is. And he took off in the middle of the morning without giving me anything to do. He said I could just go into his library and read, if I wanted to."

"That must have been when he came into town to see me."

Jenny put the spatula down, turned and regarded her worriedly. "How come?"

Janet had been wondering the very same thing ever since he'd appeared on her office doorstep. Their lunch hadn't really enlightened her. Even though Harlan had plainly stated that he wanted to discuss their future, there had been those odd undercurrents, as if he were really looking for evidence of some treachery. She couldn't share that with her daughter, so she simply said he'd wanted to talk.

"About what?" Jenny persisted. "Me?"

The last was said with a plaintive note that Janet found worrisome. "Why would you think he wanted to talk about you? Have you been making trouble out there?" When Jenny remained silent, Janet's heart sank. "Okay, what happened?"

"Nothing."

"Jenny?"

"Okay, okay. Don't bust a gut. I did make sort of a mess of his toolshed yesterday," she finally admitted.

"I see."

"But I cleaned it up," her daughter said in a rush. "I even painted it. Bright yellow, in fact. It's awesome."

Janet couldn't work up much enthusiasm over the color scheme of the toolshed, especially since Jenny herself seemed to be the reason it had needed painting.

"Why did you wreck it in the first place?" she asked, even though she thought she already knew from what Harlan had mentioned about Jenny's questions to him. "Did it have something to do with your being worried that Mr. Adams and I might be sleeping together?"

Jenny groaned and turned beet red. "He told you, didn't he? Jeez, Mom, he swore he wasn't going to blab."

"He didn't blab, at least not the way you mean. It just sort of came out in a conversation we were having."

"About the two of you?"

Janet nodded.

"So, are you?"

"Are we what?"

"Sleeping together," Jenny said impatiently. "He wouldn't say exactly."

"And neither will I," Janet said. "That's not a subject that's any of your business."

"How can you say that? He's the enemy."

Janet grinned at Jenny's determination to cling to that label. Her daughter was even more stubborn than she was. She'd conceded days ago that Harlan was no more the enemy than some descendant of Custer's might be.

"You don't believe that any more than I do," she chided.

"You're giving up?" Jenny said, staring at her incredulously. "You're not going to fight him for Lone Wolf's land?"

"I'm still researching whether there's any legal way to get the land. Besides, I told you before that I don't have evidence that Lone Wolf's father was ever on Mr. Adams's land. We may never know for sure. And the way things worked back then, it wasn't like the Comanches had deeds on file.''

''But I told him—'' Jenny turned pale. ''Whoops.''

Janet felt as if she'd been whacked over the head by a two-by-four. Of course! That explained those odd undercurrents she'd felt with Harlan. With her thoughts in turmoil, the odor of meat burning barely even registered. At the moment the fate of the hamburgers was the last thing on her mind.

''You told him what?'' she asked carefully.

''Nothing,'' Jenny muttered, backing away from the stove and clearly trying to put some distance between herself and her mother at the same time.

''Jennifer!''

''Okay, I might have let it slip that his ranch was sitting on Lone Wolf's land.''

''You might have?''

''I did, all right?'' she said belligerently. ''I don't know what difference it makes. He was going to find out sooner or later anyway.''

Janet clung to her temper by a thread. ''But it might have been nice if he found out about it from me. Now he must think I've just been playing some sort of sick game by hanging around out there. He probably thinks we're out to betray him.''

''Aren't we?'' Jenny asked simply. ''Isn't that why we're in this godawful state, instead of back home in New York, where we belong?''

With that she whirled and ran from the kitchen, leaving Janet to take the burned hamburgers from the stove. No longer the least bit interested in food, she dumped the frying pan, burgers and all, into the sink, then went out to the front porch to sit in a rocker and think.

Should she go out to White Pines first thing in the morning and tell Harlan everything? But, if he already knew most of it, why had he been trying to back her into a corner about their future earlier today? Why hadn't he been blasting her as the deceitful traitor she felt like? Would she ever understand the workings of this man's mind? Or any man's, for that matter?

And why, dear heaven, did it suddenly seem to matter so much to her that Harlan Adams not think ill of her? Was it possible that he had come to mean more to her than that elusive dream she'd formulated as a child and held on to so tightly ever since?

She could still recall Lone Wolf telling her about the Comanches known as Penateka or Honey-Eaters, who'd occupied a stretch of the Comancheria from Edwards Plateau to Cross Timbers. His telling had been further preservation of the oral history of his forefathers.

Even now she shook with indignation at his description of the 1840 meeting in San Antonio during which the Comanche leaders who'd come to discuss peace had been slaughtered in what had come to be known as the Council House Massacre. There had been nothing after that to indicate to the tribe that Texans could ever be trusted.

Slowly but surely settlers had been given more and more of the Comanche lands, until Lone Wolf's ancestors had been forced from Texas altogether. Could she ever achieve retribution for something that had occurred so long ago and even now seemed so complex? Everything she'd read indicated it would be difficult, if not impossible, to make any legal claim.

The questions kept her up most of the night. The answers didn't come at all.

In the morning, she didn't have a chance to act on any of the myriad possibilities that had occurred to her. When she and Jenny got to White Pines, Harlan was nowhere to be found. It was Cody who waited for them on the front porch.

"Come on, short stuff," he said to Jenny, who brightened immediately. "You and I are going out to look for stray calves this morning."

"Oh, wow!" Jenny said, clearly pleased to be asked to help her idol with such an important task. It was the first time Janet had seen a smile on her face since their argument the night before.

"Where's your father?" Janet asked Cody, hoping that her heart wasn't sitting in plain view on her sleeve.

He shrugged. "Beats me. He left me a note to take Jenny with me today. Didn't say where he was heading or when he'd be back. He took his plane, though. He might have had business over in Dallas or something."

"Oh." Janet fought against the tide of disappointment that washed through her as Cody headed over to the two horses he'd saddled and had tethered to a fence rail. She should have been relieved, but she wasn't. She brushed a kiss across Jenny's forehead, ignoring her daughter's embarrassed protest. "Have a good day, pumpkin. See you tonight."

"Yeah, Mom. Bye," Jenny said, already rushing off to keep up with Cody's long strides.

Feeling abandoned on all fronts, Janet stood where she was until Cody and Jenny had ridden off. Only after they'd gone did she admit to herself that she would rather have had Harlan screaming at her than ignoring her this way. There was little doubt in her mind that he'd deliberately made it a point not to be at home this morning.

Maybe he really had had unexpected business to take care of, just as Cody had suggested, she consoled herself as she drove into town. Right, she scoffed right back. Without telling Cody the details? No way. He was very careful not to step on his son's managerial toes. No, the truth of it was, he was avoiding her because his discovery of her treachery was eating at him.

She resigned herself to waiting until Harlan turned up again before settling matters between them. The delay wouldn't make much difference. She doubted she'd have any clearer an idea how to handle it hours or days from now than she did right this minute.

Harlan had spent half the night after his aborted meeting with Janet reading through every book in his library on the Comanches and their days in the southern Great Plains. Nothing he found there was conclusive proof that Janet's ancestral claim to his land was solid. In fact, it seemed to him that Lone Wolf's father had probably been a typical nomadic hunter, before being sent off to the reservation in Oklahoma.

It had been well into the wee hours of the morning when he'd decided to do a little more investigating by going to Oklahoma to see what he could discover there. His meetings with folks at the Bureau of Indian Affairs and with tribal elders who agreed to see him were inconclusive, as well. He sensed that Janet would never find the proof she sought unless she hoped to stake her claim for all Comanches and not just for her great-grandfather and his descendants.

Still, the meetings had given him much to think about, a historical perspective on his own family's actions when they'd moved to Texas to flee the war that had destroyed their home in the South. In seizing an opportunity for themselves, had they stolen it from others? He found he could understand Janet's actions far more clearly now and he could do so without feeling the rancor of betrayal.

Perhaps, if Janet ever opened up to him, they could reach some sort of compromise. In the meantime, though, he'd decided that she enriched his life too much for him to walk away without fighting for their future. It was a decision weighed and reached with years of maturity, rather than the angry, instantaneous, hot-blooded reaction he might have had a couple of decades earlier.

Also, the more he thought about the desperate plea he had made to Janet to run away with him, the more he realized that she had been exactly right to turn him down. The place to court her was right in Los Piños, in plain view. He didn't ever want a soul to think he was sneaking around with her because he wasn't proud to be seen with her. There were too many people ready with quick bias for him to be adding to that sort of rotten speculation about her morals or his own.

As soon as he'd set down his plane at the local airfield, he marched straight down Main Street, walked into her office and hauled her off to have dinner at DiPasquali's.

"Harlan," she protested, even as she hurried to keep pace with him. "What about Jenny? She's going to be waiting for me at White Pines. She'll be worried."

"I called Melissa from the airport. Jenny will have dinner with her and Cody. Sharon Lynn and baby Harlan love having her around. You can pick her up there."

She halted in her tracks and scowled at him. "Do you always have to manipulate everything to get your own way?"

He grinned unrepentantly. "Always," he assured her. "Get used to it."

He linked her arm through his and gently, but insistently, escorted her the rest of the way to the restaurant. It seemed to him her footsteps dragged a bit reluctantly, but at least she didn't bolt on him.

Inside DiPasquali's, he directed her to a table right smack in front of the window, in plain view of anybody coming or going inside the restaurant or passing by on the street outside. She regarded him with a curious look, but sat where he'd indicated.

Gina DiPasquali joined them at once with their menus, winking at Janet as she handed one to her. If he hadn't already known about their conspiracy over that dinner at Janet's, he would have wondered what the two of them were up to.

"Are you thinking of having the lasagna?" Harlan inquired innocently, his gaze fixed on Janet's face.

Gina chuckled as Janet's cheeks turned pink. "Caught you, didn't he?"

"Before he'd taken two bites," Janet admitted. "Then he rubbed it in for the rest of the evening."

"I did not," Harlan protested, feigning indignation. "But I couldn't very well let you go on thinking you'd put one over on me, though, could I? It would have set a dangerous precedent. I might never have gotten the upper hand again."

"Who says you ever had it," she shot right back. "Besides, no gentleman would have embarrassed a hostess by pointing out what he suspected. You should have been oohing and aahing over my supposed culinary skills."

Gina rolled her eyes. "If you were counting on that, I could have told you not to bother. Harlan's only a gentleman when it suits his purposes."

"Besides which, you'd have felt guilty as sin if I offered high praise for a dish you knew you hadn't prepared," he asserted. "I was just saving you that."

"How considerate," Janet retorted a trifle sourly.

Gina apparently decided to let them resolve the issue of etiquette they were debating, because she stuffed her order book back into her pocket.

"You two can sit here and battle wits from now till the cows come home," she said. "Let me choose dinner tonight, so you won't have something more to quibble about. I'll have Tony fix you something special."

"Perfect," Janet said.

Harlan decided she was apparently no more eager to choose from the menu than she was to cook in her own kitchen. It was a wonder she wasn't skin and bones.

When Gina had gone, he did an appreciative survey of Janet. Whatever her disinterest in food, she managed to have a perfectly rounded figure that could fill a man with lust. He dragged his attention away and stared at the ceiling in what was only a partially successful attempt to bring his hormones under control. The reaction only confirmed what he'd guessed earlier, that he couldn't walk away from her.

"Everything okay?" she inquired with a half smile that was all too knowing.

He caught the undisguised mirth in her eyes. "Fine," he lied. "How about you? You looked put-out when I turned up at your office a little while ago. Something on your mind?"

"Just your habit of appearing without notice and expecting me to drop everything to accompany you. Haven't you ever heard of the telephone?"

"Sure, but it's harder for you to turn me down face-to-face."

"What makes you think that?"

"Watching you stammer around for excuses a few times."

"I never stammer," she retorted irritably. "Still, I can't keep taking off at the drop of a hat, just because you get some whim to feed me."

"You have a lot of work piled up?" he inquired doubtfully.

"That's not the point."

"Sure it is. No sense in you sitting around in your office pretending to be busy, when you could be having a nice meal with me."

"What about a nice meal with my daughter?"

"Who'd cook?"

She frowned at him. "You really do have a rotten streak, Harlan Adams."

"Just speaking the gospel truth. It's not even hearsay. Don't forget I saw the state of your kitchen that night and you never even dared to put that meal on the table. Makes me wonder how the two of you have survived this long. Must have been the takeout available from all those fancy New York restaurants."

She looked a little like a chicken who'd had her feathers ruffled by that comment, but she kept her mouth clamped firmly shut. Harlan watched the temper flare in her eyes, then slowly diminish before she finally seized on another topic.

"Where did you go so early this morning?" she asked in a perfectly neutral tone.

He grinned. "So, you did miss me. I'm gratified to hear it."

"I did not say I missed you. It was a simple question, Harlan. Just a little polite conversation, okay? If it's some big secret, just say so."

He got the impression he might be pushing her a little too hard with his teasing. He opted for giving her the truth, or at least a select portion of it. "I had some unexpected business to take care of."

"I thought Cody took care of all the ranch's business these days."

"Doesn't mean I can't stick my nose into it, when I'm of a mind to," he said. "By the way, did I mention you're looking particularly beautiful today. That red blouse suits you."

"Thank you," she said, but her gaze narrowed suspiciously. "You're up to something, aren't you?"

"I could ask you the same thing with more cause," he retorted, enjoying the unmistakable guilt that darkened her eyes.

He decided there was something to be said for tormenting her. Maybe he wouldn't tell her about that trip to Oklahoma, not until she came clean with him. Surely a man was entitled to some secrets from a woman who had the ability to tie him in knots without even trying.

Gina played straight into his hands by turning up just then with a platter of antipasto and two glasses of Chianti. It got them both off the hook, which was probably to the good, he decided as he watched Janet nervously shoving a couple of olives around on her plate. Let her stew for a bit.

"You get any clients today?" he asked after a while.

She looked up, her expression revealing unmistakable gratitude for the change to a more innocuous topic. "As a matter of fact, yes. Mule came by."

Harlan's mouth gaped. "What the devil did he want?"

"That's a matter of client confidentiality," she said, obviously pleased that she'd not only stunned him, but stirred his curiosity.

"Well, I'll be damned. You sure he didn't want to get in a few quick hands of poker? He might have been running short of cash, since he's had that garage of his closed for so blasted long."

"Sorry," she said blithely. "I can't talk about it."

"Mule tells me most of his business anyway," he said, trying to coax her into telling, when he knew perfectly well that she was too ethical to ever say a word. He was enjoying aggravating her too much to stop just yet.

"Then you'll have to ask him about this," she retorted. "Now, stop prying."

"Just making polite small talk," he shot right back, echoing her earlier jab.

She rolled her eyes. He couldn't help chuckling at her exasperated expression. "You are a treasure, you know that, don't you?"

The compliment seemed to throw her off-balance. "Where did that come from?" she asked in a tone that said she didn't think she deserved it.

"Just an observation. A man's entitled to make one every now and again, isn't he?"

"Of course."

"Shall I make a few more?" he inquired, leaning forward and lowering his voice to a seductive whisper.

She swallowed hard and shook her head. "I don't think so."

He grinned. "How come?"

"Because I don't think this is the time or the place to be discussing whatever it is you have on your mind."

"Now that's an interesting bit of speculation on your part," he observed, trying to keep the amusement out of his tone. "Just what is it you think I have on my mind that would be unsuitable for discussion in a public place?"

She blushed furiously. "Never mind. Perhaps I was wrong."

Harlan shook his head. "Now, you don't strike me as a woman who admits lightly to being wrong. Maybe you ought to say what's on *your* mind. Could just be you're right on track."

"Why are you doing this?" she demanded. "A gentleman—"

"We've already established that I'm no gentleman, not when it comes to affairs of the heart, so to speak."

He allowed his gaze to sweep over her, lingering long enough to keep her color high and her nerves jittery. The game turned on him, though. The next thing he knew his own heartbeat was racing and the blood was rushing straight to a portion of his anatomy where its unmistakable effect could prove downright embarrassing. He wanted her with an urgency that drove out all other thoughts. Visions of taking her here and now took up residence in his brain and clamored for action.

Apparently he'd been wrong about one thing, though. He was just enough of a gentleman not to act on such a desperate, wicked longing. But Janet Runningbear could thank her lucky stars that he'd chosen DiPasquali's for dinner tonight instead of White Pines. He doubted he'd have been anywhere near so restrained in the privacy of his own home.

He met her gaze and thought he read a mix of passion and uncertainty in those dark brown depths. Soon, he silently promised her and himself. He would claim her soon.

As if she could read his mind, an audible sigh eased through her. A sigh of satisfaction perhaps? Or maybe anticipation? Whichever it was, Harlan could only share in the sentiment.

To him the future was as clear-cut as a pane of glass or a ten-carat diamond. Whatever Janet Runningbear's original agenda had been in coming to Los Piños, he had a feeling it was only a matter of time and subtle persuasion before he'd have her seeing the years ahead as vividly as he did.

Chapter Twelve

The bouquet of flowers that arrived in Janet's office the next morning was so huge that the only surface big enough to accommodate it was her desk. She was still staring in astonishment at the arrangement of splashy yellow mums, vivid orange tiger lilies, Texas bluebonnets and fragrant white roses when the man responsible for sending it walked in.

She didn't get it. Why was he lavishing all this attention on her, now that he knew the truth? Why had he kept so silent about what Jenny had told him? Was he planning to set her up to take a tremendous fall? If that was it, it was a pretty diabolical plan; one she couldn't imagine Harlan resorting to.

She was still trying to puzzle it out when he came up

behind her, spanned her waist with his hands, brushed aside her hair and planted a kiss on her nape.

"I see it got here," he said, sounding extremely pleased with himself.

"Just a few minutes ago," she said, unable to take her eyes off the lavish display. She couldn't quite decide whether to be awed or appalled. She settled for adding, "The flowers are beautiful."

He released her, stepped in front of her, then examined her face intently. Apparently her expression gave her away. He frowned.

"Too much?" he inquired.

"It's not that...exactly," she said, not wanting to trample on the sentiment behind the overdone gesture. She'd discovered long ago that men required all the positive reinforcement possible, if a woman expected flowers and candy not just for special occasions, but as impulsive gifts for no reason at all. This wasn't a habit she wanted to break, just to modify. And this was an improvement over that first floral excess he'd brought to the house.

She gestured helplessly at the arrangement's takeover of her desk top. "Where am I supposed to work?"

He nodded. "Definitely a problem." He settled an innocent look on her. "So, take the day off."

She couldn't help laughing at his mischievous expression and at the outrageous suggestion. "Was that why you sent such a huge bouquet, so I wouldn't be able to work?"

"Actually, no, but I'm a man who can think on his feet. I could see your dilemma right off and came up with what I consider to be the perfect solution—play hooky.''

She studied him suspiciously. ''Seems a little convenient to me that you turned up here just in time to make a suggestion like that.''

''You've obviously been hanging around with too many criminals. You lack trust.''

Janet perched on the only available corner of her desk and studied him intently. ''Okay. If—and that's a very big if—I were to take you up on your suggestion, what exactly do you have in mind?''

''Lunch,'' he said at once.

''It's barely nine-fifteen in the morning.''

''In Dallas.''

She stared at him and tried to keep her mouth from gaping. ''You want to go all the way to Dallas for lunch? Isn't that a little extravagant?''

He had a ready answer for that, too, apparently. ''We could shop,'' he said without so much as a hesitation.

''For?''

He shrugged, his expression vaguely uncertain. ''Beats me. I just figured all women loved to shop. And much as I love Los Piños, I can see that it's not exactly loaded with those fancy little designer boutiques, where a hankie costs an arm and a leg.''

''I can't afford a boutique where hankies cost a hundred times what I'd pay for a pack of tissues.''

''But I can.''

She grinned at his persistence. ''You want to fly to Dallas to buy me lunch and a hankie?''

"Or maybe a fancy outfit to wear to a party," he said, watching her with another of those exceptionally innocent expressions that wouldn't have deceived anyone with even half a brain.

Janet's gaze narrowed. "What party?"

"The one I'm throwing on Saturday night to introduce you to a few of my friends."

"Harlan, I told you I do not want you trying to drum up business for me."

He scowled, his exasperation apparent. "This isn't about business, darlin'. This is strictly personal."

For some reason she didn't find that nearly as reassuring as she should have. It struck her as being too...personal, she decided, using his own word to describe it. Too intimate. Especially given that unspoken subject hanging in the air between them. Why, why, why? she wondered again. What was he up to?

"I don't know—" she began, only to have him cut her off.

"It's no big deal," he reassured her. "There are a lot of people I owe for inviting me to dinner and stuff. I figured one big bash would take care of all those obligations. I can't have a big to-do without a proper hostess, can I?"

"And that's me?" she said skeptically. "The woman who can't cook a lick."

"I have Maritza and all of her relatives for that."

"You also have three very lovely daughters-in-law who would be happy to play hostess, I'm sure."

He waved off the suggestion. "I want a woman of my own."

She cringed at the possessive description, but let it pass. "Half the people in town barely say more than hello to me," she noted pointedly.

"That'll change when you're with me."

Knowing that he was right about that grated. "Harlan, I have to win people over myself."

"You will. I'm just opening the door, so they'll give you a chance to show 'em what a brilliant, witty, warm woman you are." He reached behind her desk and grabbed her purse. "Come on. You can think it over while we fly to Dallas."

"What about Jenny? What have you done with her since I dropped her off?"

"She's helping Melissa out with the kids today. I'm paying her ten bucks an hour to baby-sit. She says minimum wage is too cheap for the trouble those kids get into. Had to admit she was right about that."

Janet shook her head. "This is the oddest brand of punishment I've ever seen."

He shrugged. "So I'm lenient, sue me. Any more excuses?"

She was about to muster the last of her resolve and say no when she took a good, long look into his eyes. They were bright with excitement. He genuinely wanted to do this for her. How could she possibly disappoint him, when he'd already been so good to her and to Jenny? Besides, an unplanned trip to Dallas was exactly the sort of impulsive act she'd indulged in far too rarely.

"Okay, let's go for it," she said at last.

At the same time, she swore that she would do everything in her power not to take advantage of him.

Lunch was one thing. A party outfit was something else entirely. She would buy that for herself, if she could convince herself that one of the dozens of cocktail dresses already in her closet from what seemed like another lifetime wouldn't do.

For a man who claimed not to know much about shopping, Harlan guided her around the best shops in Dallas with the ease and familiarity of an extravagant tour guide. He seemed to have his heart set on a particular kind of dress and, after trying on dozens, all she knew for certain was that it wasn't baubles, bangles or beads he was looking for.

"I think I know just the place," he said at last, and led her to a boutique carrying designer Western wear. He gazed around at the fancy Western-cut shirts and rhinestone-studded jeans and nodded in satisfaction. "Yep, this is it."

Janet shook her head. "You knew all along this was what you wanted me to wear, didn't you?" she accused.

"I wasn't sure," he claimed.

"Harlan, there is no comparison between those cocktail dresses and this," she said, gesturing to the displays. "Why'd you waste three hours taking me to those stores, so I could try on silk and lace?"

"I thought all women liked to dress up in pretty clothes. Besides, I thought you might find something you couldn't resist." He shook his head. "You're a tough nut to crack, though. I never once saw a glimmer of longing in your eyes."

"Because I wore those kinds of dresses to more social functions than I care to recall back in New York. My closet is crammed with them. If I never wear another one, it will be okay with me."

He chuckled at that. "That's another thing I love about you. You've long since figured out who you are."

Janet denied his assessment with a quick shake of her head. "You're wrong. I know who I don't want to be anymore. I don't want to be a big city lawyer, living in a pressure cooker. I don't want to go to parties because I might meet someone important," she said pointedly, then added with a touch of wistfulness, "But I'm still discovering who I am."

Harlan listened to all that intently, then asked softly, "Any room in the picture for a rancher?"

The direct question took her by surprise. Her heart thumped unsteadily as she considered all the implications of what he was asking. "Maybe," she said eventually, her gaze locked with his.

"That's good enough," he said quietly. "For now."

She finally forced herself to break eye contact by feigning a sudden interest in a fancy denim outfit.

"Janet," Harlan said, drawing her attention back to him. "If there's one thing I've learned the past few years it's that life is unpredictable and often far too short. Don't get the idea I'm going to leave you much room to maneuver for long."

Her breath caught in her throat at the silky tone. "Is that a threat?"

He touched his fingers to her cheek in a light caress that set off fireworks in her midsection.

"It's a promise," he declared, then winked. "Now, try on that outfit you've been eyeing since we walked in the door. And while you're at it, take a look at that skirt and blouse with the sparkly doodads on it."

"Rhinestones?" she teased.

"That's the one. Looks perfect for square dancing."

"We're going to be dancing on Saturday?"

"Darlin', you can't have a big to-do in this part of the world and call it a party, unless there's dancing."

"I had no idea."

"That's why you have me," he reassured her. "I'm going to see to it that you fit right in in no time."

"I do so admire a man with a mission," she said as she grabbed the selected clothes off the racks and carried them into a nearby dressing room.

Inside the room, she shut the door and leaned against it, drawing in a deep breath. With every single minute she spent in Harlan Adams's company, she realized she was coming closer and closer to losing her heart. The day when she would have to choose between that and her own personal mission was clearly just around the corner.

On Saturday, Harlan fussed over every detail as the time for guests to start arriving neared. Maritza was beginning to mutter in Spanish, her tone suggesting it would be far better if he didn't try to translate. Her cousin Consuela, who'd been the original housekeeper at White Pines until Luke had lured her off to his ranch, finally backed him out the kitchen door by waving a dish towel in his face.

"Go, go. You stay out now," she ordered, barring the doorway. "You are only in the way in here."

"Damn, but you're bossy," he grumbled affectionately. "Who's running that house of Luke's? You or him?"

Her dark eyes flashed fire. "You remember that I can walk out before this affair of yours begins," she threatened, her own tone just as fond. "I will take Maritza and the others with me. How will you manage then, *señor?*"

"With my charm," he quipped.

She turned her gaze toward heaven as if praying for patience. "It will not feed this crowd you have invited," she reminded him. "Now, go and talk with your sons or play with your grandbabies."

"I'll go out and check to see if the tent's set up right," he said.

"No," she ordered at once. "The men have everything under control." She tilted her head at him. "I do not recall you making such a fuss over details in the past. This party is important to you?"

He nodded, feeling sheepish. "Silly, huh? We must have thrown a hundred parties in this house, but this is the first time I've ever been a wreck."

Consuela's expression sobered at once. "It is because you no longer have Mary by your side," she said sorrowfully. "I should have thought, Señor Harlan. You must miss her very much at a time like this."

That was part of it, he supposed. But he'd come to terms with his loss in the past few months. Though he was likely to miss Mary until the end of his days, he had moved on. No, this sense that he was standing at the edge of a precipice and that the slightest misstep would send him over was due to another woman entirely.

"No," he corrected softly. "It is because I want everything to be perfect tonight."

Consuela's eyes widened. "For the *señorita,* yes?" At his startled look, she explained, "Rosa told me she has seen you together in town many times and then Luke and Jessie described meeting her. They say your eyes light up when you are in the same room. You care for this woman?"

He nodded, even though that was a pale description of his feelings. "Deeply," he admitted.

"Then Maritza and I will see that this party impresses her. Leave it to us, okay?"

He grinned. "Do I have any choice?"

"No," she conceded, and disappeared into the kitchen from which she had just banished him.

Left at loose ends, he paced. When that failed to calm him, he retreated to his office and fiddled with papers, none of which caught his full attention. He was trying for the third time to add up a simple column of figures when he realized he was no longer alone. He glanced up and found not one, but six pairs of prying eyes studying him with amusement.

"What's the matter with the bunch of you?" he grumbled, staring sourly at his sons and their wives. If he could have kept them away from this event, he would have, but he hadn't wanted to send the wrong message to Janet. He was very aware of how sensitive she was about not being accepted in Los Piños, despite the cavalier attitude she had expressed on the subject.

"We heard you were driving the entire staff nuts," Luke said. "Consuela thought you might need company."

"Consuela is a busybody." He noticed Jordan and Cody rolling their eyes. "And you two can be uninvited, you know."

"Us?" Jordan said innocently, exchanging a look with his younger brother. "What did we do?"

"We're giving him a taste of his own medicine," Cody retorted, clearly undaunted by the threat. "Looks like he can't take it."

Harlan heard the sound of footsteps clattering down the stairs. "Aren't those your little hellions I hear?" he demanded. "Damn, but they make a racket. Can't you control them?"

"Those are your precious grandchildren," Luke corrected. "And you're the one who said you wanted this to be a family event. How come, Daddy? You have big plans for tonight? Maybe an announcement of some kind?"

Harlan was startled by the suggestion, even though he could see how they might have leapt to that conclusion. "Don't go getting ideas. This shindig's just to let Janet get to know the family and some of my friends."

"How big's the guest list?" Jordan prodded, his expression entirely too smug.

"Two hundred, okay?" Harlan retorted, frowning at him. "Once I got started, I figured I might as well invite everybody at once."

"I hope Janet's not expecting an intimate little gathering," Jessie said worriedly. "I'll never forget that birthday party you threw for me when I was first married to Erik. I'd never seen that many people gathered together outside of a church revival in my entire life."

"Well, we'll know soon enough," Kelly stated. "She and Jenny are just pulling up." She grinned at her father-in-law. "Did you tell her to come early to play hostess?"

Harlan shook his head in disgust at their teasing. "Never mind what I told her," he said as he strode past them.

"He must not think we're up to the responsibility," Kelly said to Jessie and Melissa. "Think we should stage a protest?"

"I'm for it," Melissa teased.

Harlan turned back and glared at the lot of them. "If you all don't behave tonight, I'm disowning every one of you."

"I win!" Cody said with a whoop.

Harlan scowled at his youngest. "Win what?"

"We placed bets on how long it would take you to threaten to disown us. I figured less than ten minutes. Luke and Jordan thought you'd hold your temper longer."

"I was counting on Janet being here to keep him in line," Luke explained.

"Out of the will, every one of you," Harlan declared as he walked off and left them laughing.

Only after he was out of their eyesight did he allow himself to smile.

Harlan must have invited everyone within a hundred-mile radius, Janet decided as she stared at the throng of people filling their plates at the heavily laden buffet tables.

As if he sensed that she might be overwhelmed, he had stuck close to her side ever since her arrival, silencing gossip with a frown, introducing her to people who could bring her their legal business, shielding her from his sons' excessive teasing.

He'd left her just a moment before to greet the governor, promising to bring him back to meet her. The governor, for heaven's sake! At what Harlan referred to as a little backyard barbecue. Obviously he took such illustrious guests in stride.

To her, the sheer size of the event was daunting without even taking into account the importance of some of the guests. Her ex-husband would have had whiplash from looking this way and that to be sure he didn't miss anybody. The fancy New York parties they'd attended had been nothing compared to this assembly of Texas's rich and powerful.

"A little daunting, isn't it?" Jessie inquired, magically appearing by her side just when Janet was beginning to feel exactly that way.

"It's second nature to him, isn't it?" she replied, watching the ease with which Harlan escorted the governor from cluster to cluster. As many parties as she'd been to, she'd never been entirely comfortable with the small talk required.

"You wouldn't have thought that, if you'd seen him earlier," Jessie revealed. "He was like a kid throwing his first party and terrified nobody would come. Of course, in his case, I think you're the only guest he's been really worried about."

Janet couldn't get over the idea that Harlan might have suffered a bad case of stage fright. "He was nervous?" she asked incredulously.

Jessie nodded. "Because of you. He really wanted tonight to be special for you." She studied Janet intently. "Are you two involved? I mean, happily-ever-after involved."

Janet evaded a direct answer by asking a question of her own, "What does he say?"

"Not a darn thing, really. It's driving all of us crazy." She grinned. "I figure it serves Luke and his brothers right. On the other hand, I want to be in on the secret."

"There is no secret," Janet assured her.

Jessie's expression turned serious. "If he asks you to marry him, what will you say?"

Janet swallowed hard. It was clear that Jessie felt her question wasn't nearly as premature as Janet hoped it was. "I can't answer that," she said. To soften the response, she added, "And even if I could, you're not the one I'd be telling. Harlan would be the first to have an answer."

Jessie nodded approvingly. "Good. Now I know that all the bullying from these Adams men won't force you into a corner." She grinned. "It takes a strong woman to put up with them. I think you'll do just fine."

"Thanks for the vote of confidence," Janet said. "But sometimes trying to say no to Harlan is like swimming in quicksand."

"You ever need a lifeline, just let me know," Jessie offered. "The same with Kelly or Melissa. We've all been there." She glanced up and caught sight of Harlan approaching with the governor at the same time Janet did. "Whoops, I'm out of here. I voted for his opponent. I'd hate to have to admit that in front of Harlan."

Janet was still chuckling when Harlan reached her. She acknowledged the introduction to the governor and his wife with a smile and sufficient small talk to cover her nervousness. Fortunately, the band struck up a slower tune just then.

"That's my cue," the governor said, beaming at his wife. "Shall we?" As they headed for the dance floor, he said, "Call my office next week. I'd like to talk with you a bit about your interest in Native American affairs."

Janet stared after him openmouthed. "How did he know about that?"

Harlan shrugged. "I might have mentioned it. All that talk about Lone Wolf and his ancestors led me to think you might have a particular interest in the subject."

As if he thought he might have already said too much, he glanced toward the crowded dance floor that had been set up under the stars. "How about it? You willing to risk a turn around the floor with me?"

The request didn't give her time to wonder how a few comments about Lone Wolf had led Harlan to guess how deep her interest in Native Americans ran. Before she could even form a question, she was in his arms and they were swaying to the soft music.

The feel of his body pressed against hers made every inch of her flesh tingle. With her head tucked against his shoulder, she felt warm and secure and desired. His heat surrounded her, making her senses swim.

Suddenly she was no longer aware of anything but the provocative rhythm of the music and the feel of his muscles playing against her own. She could hear the steady sound of his heart pounding, feel the quickening of his pulse. A desperate hunger began to build deep inside her, a hunger that was clearly matched in the man who held her so tightly.

"You'll stay the night?" he asked out of the blue, his gaze searching hers.

"Jenny," she said, unable to manage another single word.

He nodded his understanding of her concern. "Not to worry. I'll speak to Cody. Melissa will think up an excuse to have her baby-sit. Will that do?"

"Yes," she whispered, sighing as she settled her head against his shoulder. She was grateful for his consideration, anxious to get this entire crowd on its way before she had time for second thoughts.

He leaned back and gazed down at her. "You want me to send everybody packing as badly as I want to do it?" he inquired, a teasing glint in his eyes.

"Yes," she admitted. "Isn't that terrible, especially when you've gone to all this trouble?"

"Wanting it isn't so bad," he claimed. "We'll just have to think of it as a test of character that we don't act on it." He winked at her. "Besides, a little anticipation isn't all bad. It'll just make the rest of the night all the sweeter."

Janet regarded him skeptically. It seemed to her the next few hours were going to be the longest of her entire life. And if Harlan had a brain in his head, he wouldn't give her anywhere near that long to reconsider the decision she'd just reached in the provocative circle of his arms.

He leaned down then to whisper in her ear. "Don't look so impatient, darlin'. You'll be giving folks ideas about what's on your mind."

"No question about that," Luke said impudently as he tapped his father on the shoulder. "I'm cutting in before you two make a spectacle of yourselves."

"Go away," Harlan said, refusing to release her.

Janet chuckled as the two of them stared each other down. "I think Luke has the right idea," she said, slipping out of Harlan's embrace. "Go dance with somebody else for a while."

Harlan frowned at his oldest son. "You'll pay for this," he muttered irritably, but he did start off. He hadn't gone more than half a dozen steps before he turned back to Janet. "You and I have a date, darlin'. Don't be forgetting it."

"Not a chance," she promised.

She looked up to find Luke chuckling. "What?" she demanded.

"Another five seconds I'd have had to hose the two of you down."

"I'm beginning to see why your father finds you so irritating," she muttered.

He laughed out loud at that. "Jessie was right."

"About?"

"You'll fit in just fine."

The approval behind the comment stayed with Janet for the rest of the seemingly endless evening. She was glad that Luke and Jessie thought she'd be right for Harlan. She couldn't help wondering, though, how they'd feel if they discovered what had originally brought her to Texas. Would they be as open and generous then? Or would they do everything in their power to see that she and Harlan never spent another single second alone together?

Chapter Thirteen

"We'll all meet here for a late breakfast," Harlan said to Jenny as she prepared to leave with Cody and Melissa and their kids after the party. He'd been trying to shoo people off for an hour now, to little avail. His sons particularly showed no inclination to go.

To Janet's surprise, though, Jenny didn't seemed particularly thrown by the change in plans. She was probably thrilled to be spending the night under Cody's roof. Fortunately her daughter had missed the earlier exchange of winks between Cody and his brothers when they'd learned that Harlan was sending Jenny home with Cody and his crew.

"You'll be back then, too, Mom?" Jenny asked sleepily as she climbed into Cody's car.

Janet nodded. "I'll be here," she promised.

Jenny yawned. "Okay. See you."

A moment later they were gone and Janet's heart climbed straight into her throat at the look of pure longing in Harlan's eyes. Despite the irreversible commitment she'd made to stay, despite her own yearning to make love to this incredibly gentle, thoughtful man, she was more nervous than an innocent bride on her wedding night.

She still had so many questions about why he seemed to have forgiven her for what must have seemed to him a hiding of the truth at least. That he still hadn't mentioned what Jenny had told him kept her from relaxing and falling entirely under his spell. She kept waiting for him to reel her in and then turn on her when she least expected it.

"What about the others?" she asked, delaying their return to the house.

His gaze never left her face. "What others?" he murmured distractedly, his attention clearly riveted on her.

"Jordan and Kelly, for instance," she said, though she was a bit distracted herself by the intensity of his gaze and the electricity arcing between them.

He stroked a finger along her cheek. "They've gone home. Slipped away a while ago, in fact."

Janet swallowed hard before managing to add, "And Luke and Jessie?"

"Upstairs in their suite." Her expression must have given away her trepidation, because he quickly added, "It's at the opposite end of this big old place from mine. Think of it as being like a fancy hotel. You wouldn't think twice about who was down the hall."

"But this room is occupied by your son and his family, not strangers."

He shrugged off her concern. "I promise you it's not a problem."

Janet disagreed. "How will they feel when they find out I've stayed the night?"

"For one thing, I don't think any of them had a doubt in the world that you would be here come morning. Besides that, you seem to be forgetting whose house this is."

"Hardly."

"Okay, but whatever Luke's opinion might be, he'll keep it to himself."

Janet chuckled at the unlikelihood of that. "Are we talking about the same Luke?"

"Stop fussing," he soothed, cupping her face in his hands. "If you want to put this off, just say the word. You'll have your own room for the night. I can even fix you up on a different floor, if you'd prefer. Give you a key for the lock, too, if it'll make you feel better."

She wrestled with the offer. Eventually, longing and a deep sense of inevitability overcame doubt. With Jenny staying at Cody's overnight, there might never be another opportunity like this one.

She reached up and covered his hands with her own. Her gaze locked with his. "If I stay here tonight, it will be with you."

Rather than seeming relieved, he tensed as questions darkened his eyes. "If? You aren't seriously thinking of driving back into town, are you?"

She tilted her head. A smile tugged at her lips at the stark disappointment in his expression. She had another alternative in mind, one with which she was far more comfortable.

"I was thinking I'd have you take me," she said. She lowered her voice to a coaxing note. "My house might be a half hour from here, but it is totally deserted." Unspoken was the fact that there would be no ghosts in the bed or prying family members down the hall.

The tension in his shoulders eased the instant he caught her meaning. "Well, why didn't you say so?" he said, grinning. "I'll get my car keys."

"Mine are in my purse," she said, already reaching for them and handing them over. "Besides, with only my car parked out front, no one will ever guess you're there. No gossip."

"Better yet."

They rounded the house, laughing like a couple of kids sneaking off to make out. Harlan gunned the engine in a way that would have had Mule sulking for a month about his disrespect for what the mechanic had declared to be an almost-classic car.

Then he shot down the lane and away from White Pines as if he'd been celibate for a decade and had finally discovered he was about to get lucky. Janet found his eagerness both touching and very arousing.

The drive into Los Piños seemed to take an eternity, especially after Harlan placed her hand on his rock-hard thigh and covered it with his own. So much heat, she thought as her senses spun wildly. So much strength. So much barely contained passion.

His blatant desire fueled hers, until by the time they reached her house, the last of her uncertainties had been stripped away. They rushed through her front door, barely taking the time for Harlan to kick it shut behind him before he dragged her into his arms. He kissed her with all of the pent-up hunger that had been held in check on the dance floor, on the long drive and for who knew how long before.

The kiss was commanding and all-consuming, wiping out every thought except for some primitive understanding of its wicked effect on her senses. Never in her life had she experienced such raw, untamed lust. She was suddenly trembling from head to toe with anticipation.

She was fumbling with the buttons on Harlan's shirt just as urgently as he was stripping away the blouse they'd searched all over Dallas to find just yesterday. Then his mouth was covering first one breast, then the other, teasing, suckling in a way that sent shock waves ricocheting through her.

His skin was on fire beneath her touch, but her own was hotter. The caress of his tongue cooled, then inflamed, then cooled again in a devastating cycle. A moan of pure pleasure escaped, shattering their previously silent, passionate duet.

The sound brought his head up, leaving her feeling bereft. As if he had suddenly found his bearings, he tucked her tightly against his chest and sucked in a deep, calming breath.

"Whoa, darlin'," he murmured softly, as if gentling a skittish mare.

"No," she pleaded. "Don't stop."

He chuckled at the urgency in her tone. "I will not make love to you on the floor in the foyer," he said. "Not that I'm entirely sure I can get us both out of this tangle we've made of our clothes and into the bedroom."

If that was the only delay, Janet was more than willing to help. She shucked what was left of her clothing, kicked it aside and headed down the hallway stark naked. Only when she realized Harlan hadn't followed did she turn back. He was staring after her, looking stunned. The thoroughly masculine appreciation in his eyes made her knees go weak.

"You take my breath away," he said in a hoarse whisper.

"Ditto," she said in a voice only faintly louder. "If you get over here, though, I'll give you mouth-to-mouth resuscitation."

Amusement danced in his eyes at that. "You certified?"

"No," she admitted, then grinned. "I'll need lots and lots of practice."

Practically before the words were out of her mouth, he had joined her, scooping her up and carrying her into the bedroom with long, anxious strides.

"Then by all means, let's get to it," he said, lowering her to the bed, then settling down beside her atop the thick comforter.

The break had allowed just enough time for ardor to cool. To Janet's astonishment, it took little more than a sweeping caress of her bare hip with callused fingers to return it to a fever pitch.

But Harlan was clearly in no hurry now that they'd made it this far. He seemed intent on making each response linger, then build to a shattering crescendo before trying something new. In her head, Janet knew that this was the same body she'd lived with all her life, but under his gentle, tormenting ministrations it seemed entirely new and heart-stoppingly responsive.

She was filled with astonishment over each exquisite, devastating sensation. And when every nerve was vibrantly alive, when he finally, at long last, entered her with a slow, tantalizing thrust, she felt as if she'd finally discovered the true meaning of joy.

As their bodies played out this timeless ritual, over and over through the night, perfecting it, elaborating on it, exploring its every nuance, she wondered if she'd ever been alive before she met Harlan Adams or if she'd just been existing in some half-awake state, waiting for this moment.

Discovering such passion deep within herself should have been exhilarating, but in the silvery, moonlit darkness just before dawn broke she was overcome by an agony of indecision. She tried to compare these new, barely tested feelings for the man sprawled out half on top of her, his hand possessively circling her breast, with older loyalties to the grandfather she had adored.

If there hadn't been such a history in her family of mistakes, of choosing mates so unwisely, perhaps she could have reached a different decision. But neither

her father nor her first husband had understood this gut-deep need she had to discover the Comanche side of her heritage. She doubted Harlan would be any different, especially when he realized that part of that discovery meant righting a century-old wrong if there was any legal means at all to do so.

Sighing, she resolved that this night would never be repeated. She knew with everything in her that it was a decision Harlan would never understand, one he would fight with all of his incomparable powers of persuasion. She also knew it was the only one she could make.

And knowing that broke her heart.

Harlan was the kind of man who usually snapped awake in an instant. He'd never had much interest in lingering in bed when there were chores to do and a ranch to run. Maybe the trait had been born of necessity decades ago, but it had become a habit he'd had no reason to break, not even when the whole day stretched out emptily ahead of him.

This morning, though, he seemed to be easing back into consciousness, sensation by sensation. First it was the heat that tugged at his senses. Then it was the sweet, sweet smell of some light-as-air flowery scent, layered with an undertone of dark, musky sensuality. And then, dear heaven, it was the soft-as-satin brush of skin against skin, a teasing caress that had his blood pumping so hard and fast he thought his heart might flat-out explode in his chest.

That woke him, all right! His eyes snapped open to gaze straight into sleepy, dark eyes that struck him as far more troubled than they ought to be after such an incredible night.

"You're looking mighty serious," he said, brushing Janet's hair back over her shoulders so he could drink his fill of the sight of those rose-tipped breasts. The peaks pebbled at once, even under such an off-hand caress. He might have lingered longer, intensified his touch, had Janet's gaze not seemed so fraught with worry.

"Regrets?" he asked.

"None," she swore.

Harlan wasn't convinced. "You sure?"

"I could never regret what happened between us last night," she said more firmly.

Though he was still doubtful, he decided he'd just have to take her at her word. "Then I think we ought to talk about making it permanent."

This time there was no mistaking the alarm that flared in her eyes.

"No," she whispered, touching a finger to his lips. "Please, don't say any more."

He couldn't take rejection so easily, not when he had his heart set on spending his future with this woman, not when he knew without a trace of doubt that deep inside that was what she wanted, too. He suspected he even knew what was preventing her from accepting his proposal.

"You don't even want me saying that I love you?" he said, keeping his tone light. "You don't want to hear that I won't settle for anything less than making you my wife, not after last night?"

A tear slid slowly down her cheek, even as she declined his proposal for a second time.

"I can't," she whispered.

"Of course you can," he insisted just as adamantly. "There's nothing to stop you, except some foolish willfulness on your part."

He knew as soon as the words were out of his mouth that they had been exactly the wrong thing to say. Whatever she was struggling with—and he was certain now that he knew what it was—he shouldn't have dismissed it as foolish or willful. A milewide stubborn streak would kick in over words like that. His own certainly would have.

"I'm sorry. I shouldn't have said that," he apologized at once.

"No," she said stiffly, retreating as far from him in the bed as she could and surrounding herself with layers of covers despite the room's more than comfortable temperature. "You shouldn't have."

Because he needed time to rein in his temper, Harlan stood and searched for his pants. When he'd yanked them on, he returned to sit opposite her on the edge of the bed.

"Can we discuss this?"

"I don't see why you'd want to," she said dully.

"Because this is too important for you to leap to a snap decision that could affect the rest of both of our lives, to say nothing of Jenny's," he explained, fighting to keep his tone even. "You know I care for her as if she were one of my own. You also know I've been a good influence on her."

She shot him a stubborn scowl. "I'm not going to get married again because Jenny needs a father."

"Then how about because you need a husband who loves you, almost as much as I need a wife who'll make me feel alive the way you did in this bed last night, the way you have every day since we met? Can you deny you felt the same way?"

"No, of course not. I would never lie to you about something that important," she told him. "But I came here to find myself. You're such a strong man. From all I've heard, your first wife doted on you. You were her first and only priority. I'm afraid I'd turn out to be just like her, that I'd lose myself in being Mrs. Harlan Adams, rather than Janet Running-bear, a Comanche lawyer in search of her roots."

"It's the last that's important, isn't it?" he said, experiencing the bitter taste of defeat in his mouth. "It's this thing you have about your great-grand-father."

Her gaze narrowed. "What if it is?"

"Why don't you tell me what really brought you to Texas?" he commanded.

Her gaze faltered. "I've told you a hundred different ways," she said. "You haven't been listening."

"You want to know what I hear? I hear you denying yourself a future you want because of some crazy notion that won't ever pan out the way you want it to."

She frowned at that. "Don't be so certain of that, Harlan. There's very little I can't accomplish if I set my mind to it. I won't let you or my feelings for you stand in my way. I can't allow that to happen. I will never be like Mary, so you might as well accept that and move on.''

It was quite likely the only argument she might have made that he didn't have a ready answer for. Words were too easy for a fear like that, especially when he couldn't deny that Mary had given up a part of herself the day she became his wife.

He resigned himself to taking a little time to show Janet that that had been Mary's choice, not his. He was ready and eager to have a strong and independent woman at his side. He was no young kid who'd mistake independence of spirit with a lack of love.

Patience, unfortunately, was not one of his virtues. More, he suspected that that would solve only part of the problem. Janet was still struggling with her conscience over her desire to get her hands on the land that she felt had belonged to her ancestors.

Until she could tell him about that herself, until they could work it through together, it would always stand between them and happiness. She'd almost said the words a moment ago, he was sure of it, but something had kept her silent. Whether it was fear of his reaction or a desire not to hurt him, he couldn't be sure.

''Okay,'' he said eventually. ''I'll let it slide for now, if I must.''

He walked around to the other side of the bed where she still sat huddled under the covers. He determinedly tucked a finger under her chin and tilted her face up until their eyes clashed.

''But I won't give up on us. I'll pester you until you see what I see, that we belong together.''

A clearly reluctant smile tugged at the corners of her mouth. "That ought to scare the hell out of me," she said, then gave a little shrug of resignation. "But for some crazy reason, it doesn't."

"That's because you know I'm right," he said with satisfaction.

"I do not," she insisted.

"Argue all you want, but the end result will still be the same," he informed her. "Now get dressed so we can sneak back to White Pines before the whole gang figures out we're missing."

"It would serve you right," she muttered as she strolled off to the shower. "You're the one they'd taunt unmercifully. They're very polite to me."

"They won't be, once they know you're going to be family."

"I am not going to be..." she shouted, then sighed audibly. "Oh, never mind."

Harlan grinned as the bathroom door slammed behind her. Yes, indeed, no matter what she thought, no matter what kind of struggle she put up, it was only a matter of time.

Facing the entire Adams clan around the breakfast table—except for the youngest babies, who were being watched upstairs—was a heck of a lot more intimidating than their first meeting had been, Janet decided after several awkward minutes ticked by. Their fascinated gazes kept shifting from her to Harlan and back again. Only Jenny and the older grandchildren seemed oblivious to the undercurrents. Their unrestrained chatter was all that made the situation bearable.

The minute everyone had finished eating, Harlan said, "I had Consuela's brother put up the wading pool out back. Jenny, why don't you take the little ones out to play in that and keep an eye on them?"

Jenny surveyed him speculatively. "My usual rates?"

"Yes, you little entrepeneur," he said with contradictory fondness. "I'll pay you your usual rates."

"Great! I'll be able to buy more CDs, if we ever get to a town with a decent music store," she said with a pointed look in Janet's direction.

"Maybe next weekend," Janet replied distractedly. She was too worried about the inquisitive expressions on Cody's, Jordan's and Luke's faces to pay much attention to Jenny's normal grumbling about the lack of shopping in Los Piños.

The reply seemed to satisfy her daughter, because she took off readily with the younger children.

"Well?" Luke said, his gaze fixed on his father.

Harlan tried to stare him down. "Well, what?"

"Isn't there something you two want to tell us?"

"No," Harlan and Janet replied in chorus.

Luke and Jessie exchanged a look filled with amusement that was promptly caught by the others.

"You know something, don't you?" Cody guessed. "Come on, big brother, share."

Harlan's gaze narrowed. "I don't know what you think you know, Lucas," he said, "but if you've got any decency in you, you'll keep it to yourself."

"He has a point," Jessie said, laughter dancing in her eyes. "I mean, we don't know for sure where they were going when they went sneaking off in the middle of the night."

Janet groaned and buried her face in her hands, sure that her complexion must be a fiery shade of red. "That's it. I'm out of here," she declared, shoving her chair back and practically racing from the room.

"Now look what you've done," Harlan chided, sending his own chair scooting across the floor with a clatter. "When I get back, I want you out of here. Maybe the whole blasted lot of you ought to think about moving to Arizona or Montana, anywhere that's far away from here."

If she hadn't been so embarrassed, Janet might have chuckled at his blustery tone. As it was, she just wanted to disappear herself. She was already outside when he caught up with her.

"I'm sorry," he said. "You know what big mouths they have. I told you so myself before we came back here this morning."

"It's not that," she said miserably. "It's just so sweet the way they tease you. I know they wouldn't do that, if they didn't want something to happen between you and me. I feel as if I'm letting all of you down."

"Only for the moment," he reminded her with that trace of stubbornness that proved he still hadn't accepted that her no meant an emphatic *no*.

She lifted her chin and leveled a look straight into his eyes. "No, Harlan. Not just for the moment. I meant what I said back at my house. There is no future for us, not unless you mean it to be no more than friendship.''

''I won't settle for that,'' he said with surprisingly little rancor. She knew why when he added, ''And in time, neither will you.''

Chapter Fourteen

Jenny's presence was the only thing that gave Harlan any peace of mind at all in the days after Janet had fled from White Pines. The fact that she continued to turn up every morning reassured him that there was hope. It enabled him to be patient.

Not that the teenager had suddenly turned into a saint or even a staunch advocate of his relationship with her mother, but she was showing signs of weakening. Her belligerence was sported more for effect than any real attitude on her part. He decided one afternoon to call her on it.

She'd thrown a fit not an hour before over some inconsequential task he'd asked her to do. She'd saddled Misty after that and taken off. He guessed he'd find her at the creek.

Sure enough, she was sitting on the grassy bank, her bare feet dangling in the cool water.

"If you wanted to come down here, all you had to do was ask," he said, dropping to the ground beside her.

She regarded him with disbelief. "You'd have let me come?"

"You know I would. You also know I would have come along. You just figured you ought to raise a ruckus so I wouldn't get too used to the more mellow Jenny, isn't that right?"

She slanted a look at him. "You think you're pretty smart, don't you?"

"I know I am. The question is, are you ready to admit it?"

She sighed heavily. "If you're so smart, how come Mom's dropping me off at the end of the lane again? It's her idea this time," she added, so there would be no mistake.

"Because she's sorting through some things."

"She's behaving like a ninny, you mean."

He grinned. "Is that what I mean?"

"Seems that way to me." She met his gaze evenly. "Are you in love with her?"

"Don't you think that's between her and me?"

"Not if I have to live with her while you two are figuring things out. I think I deserve to know what's going on." She shot him a sly look. "I could help you, you know. Mom listens to me."

Harlan hid a smile. "Is that so? What would your intercession on my behalf cost me?"

Jenny blinked. "Hey, wait a minute," she protested. "That's not the kind of thing I'd charge you for."

"Then that would be a first," he said dryly.

"Look, you don't want my help, it's no skin off my nose. You don't seem to be doing so great on your own, though."

"Trust me," he said. "I can handle this without any help from you." He studied her curiously. "But can I assume from what you're saying that you would approve of your mother and me getting married?"

She looked reluctant to make that big an admission, but finally she shrugged. "I suppose it would be okay."

He grinned. "Thanks for the endorsement."

"Would it mean I could stop doing chores and get an allowance?"

"I doubt it."

"Oh." She regarded him intently. "But you would want me around, right?"

"You bet," he said. "It's definitely a package deal. You comfortable with having me as a stepdaddy?"

To his astonishment, Jenny shifted and threw her arms around his neck. She didn't say a word, but the dampness of fresh tears on his neck told him all he needed to know. He had himself a daughter.

Janet was feeling besieged. Not by Harlan, bless his heart. To her surprise he was giving her all the space she'd claimed to crave. No, it was his family that wouldn't leave her in peace.

Every son, every daughter-in-law made some excuse or another to pay a call, to proclaim all of Harlan's virtues, to try to wheedle from her a reason for her reluctance to accept the proposal, which they had somehow discovered he'd made. She had the same answer for each of them: "Does your father know you're here?"

And when the reply was consistently no, she suggested that they talk with him if they had questions about the relationship. "He knows why I won't marry him," she repeated over and over.

Unfortunately, Jessie wasn't as easily dissuaded as the others. She popped in two weeks after that disgraceful scene Janet had caused by running out of the dining room at White Pines. The minute she'd walked through the door, she settled into a seat opposite Janet and showed no inclination at all to leave.

"I'm not going to talk about it," Janet declared for what must have been the hundredth time, hoping just this once to stop any questions before they started.

Jessie nodded. "That's understandable," she soothed.

It was, perhaps, the hundredth time Janet had heard that, too. Everyone who'd dropped by had said the same thing, then proceeded to butt in just the same.

"It's private," Jessie added, indicating a deeper understanding than most.

"Exactly."

"Harlan's probably done more than enough bullying himself without the rest of us getting in on the act."

"Precisely," Janet said.

To her relief, Jessie appeared willing to give up. She even stood, to indicate an imminent departure.

"Let's go to Dolan's and have a milk shake," she suggested.

Janet blinked. "What?"

"A thick, chocolate milk shake," Jessie added temptingly. "Come on. I never get anything like that at the ranch. Consuela's a great cook, but lately she's constantly worried about killing Luke with too much fat. There hasn't been so much as a pint of ice cream in the house in months. I have to sneak over here to Los Piños to get a milk shake, if I want one."

"And just this morning you decided you had a hankering for one and drove...what? Two hours? Three, just to get one?" Janet said skeptically, not believing for a minute that Jessie couldn't have whipped one up right in her own kitchen if she'd really wanted to.

"It's amazing the cravings that come on when a woman least expects them," Jessie said. "Chocolate milk shakes..." Her expression turned innocent. "A man, same difference. Once the idea's planted in your head, you might as well give in to it."

That sneaky little reference to men triggered all of Janet's alarm systems. "Are you suggesting that I should go ahead and marry Harlan, because he's like some sort of addiction I won't be able to break?"

Jessie regarded her with another innocent look. "I was talking about milk shakes. You're the one who brought up marriage." She tilted her head inquiringly. "Has it been on your mind a lot lately?"

"If I didn't like you so much, I'd tell you to go fly a kite," Janet muttered, but she stood. "As it is, though, now you've got me craving a milk shake, too. Let's go."

They walked down the block to Dolan's Drugstore and headed for the counter. Melissa popped out of the store room. She'd worked there before her marriage to Cody and still filled in several days a week to keep from going stir-crazy on the ranch.

"Hey, you two, what brings you in in the middle of the morning?" Melissa asked. "Jessie, I didn't know you were coming to Los Piños today."

Janet thought the greeting sounded suspiciously cheery, as if they'd plotted this little gathering. When Kelly strolled in not five minutes later, she knew it.

"Okay, what's going on?" she demanded.

"That's what we want to know," Kelly said, propping her elbows on the counter and leaning forward intently. "Harlan's been grumbling like an old bear for the last week. Jordan, Cody and Luke are practically busting with curiosity, but he refuses to say a single word to any of them. Cody told Jordan you've been dropping Jenny off at the end of the lane again."

"I had no idea everyone was so fascinated with my habits," Janet said irritably.

As if she sensed that Janet was about ready to bolt, Jessie laid a soothing hand on top of hers. "Look, we all like you and we love Harlan. You seem to make him happy. He's crazy about Jenny. I doubt the two of you would have gone sneaking off and tearing down that lane in the middle of the night, if you weren't more than fond of him. So, what's the deal?''

"It's complicated," Janet summarized.

"Nothing's too complicated it can't be worked out, if two people love each other," Melissa declared, distributing milk shakes without even being asked. "I can vouch for that."

"Me, too," Jessie said.

"And me," Kelly added. "We had three of the most reluctant bridegrooms in Texas and look at us now. We're all deliriously happy."

"Well, most of the time," Jessie amended. "After all, those Adams stubborn streaks didn't vanish overnight."

Two "Amens" greeted the comment.

"Anyway," Melissa said. "You clearly have Harlan in the palm of your hand, yet you're throwing away the chance to marry him. How come? Is Jessie wrong? Don't you care about him?"

"I love him," Janet forced herself to admit to these three women who were clearly so concerned with their father-in-law's future that they'd ganged up on her. "That's why I can't marry him."

"Huh?" Kelly said blankly. It was echoed by the others.

Janet pushed aside her practically untouched shake. "I can't explain. Not to you, anyway. I can't even make myself tell Harlan all of it."

"Are you still married or something?" Melissa asked, eyes wide.

Janet grinned. "No, it's nothing like that."

"Then you can work it out," Jessie said confidently. "Just tell him what's on your mind. Harlan loves to fix things up for the people he cares about."

Kelly nodded. "He doesn't lay on some heavy guilt trip like a lot of men would. He just takes care of things."

Janet wondered if she could bring herself to tell Harlan that she had wanted the very land he was living on. If she did, would he ever believe that she was marrying him for any reason except to get her hands on that land? It didn't seem likely.

"At least think about it," Jessie prodded. "You won't regret marrying Harlan."

That had never been her fear, Janet thought. She was far more concerned that Harlan would regret marrying her.

That night, now fully aware that her every move was being scrutinized by fascinated relations, she drove all the way up the lane at White Pines to the house to pick up Jenny. She had almost managed to convince herself to lay all of her cards on the table and tell Harlan everything. She would test Jessie and Kelly's theory that Harlan would somehow make everything right and forgive her.

When she arrived, he was nowhere in sight. Maritza answered the doorbell.

"You are here for Jenny, *sí?* She will be back soon, I think."

"Actually I'd like to speak with Mr. Adams if he's available," she said.

"He's in his office. Come, I will show you."

She led Janet down the hall and pointed to a heavily carved door. "In there. You would like me to tell him you are here?"

"No, I'll knock. Thanks, Maritza."

She stood outside the door for several minutes summoning up her courage before finally rapping softly. "Harlan?"

"Janet, is that you? Come on in," he called out so eagerly that she was immediately consumed by another bout of guilt.

He was on his feet and halfway across the room by the time she had the door open. His expression made her heart skitter wildly. There was so much hope there. So much love.

"I wasn't expecting to see you today. You've been making yourself scarce."

"I had some thinking to do." She looked into eyes so blue they reminded her of the summer sky. "Thank you for letting me do it in peace."

He looked as if he wanted to reach for her, but he shoved his hands into his pockets instead. "Reach any conclusions?"

"Just one, thanks to Jessie, Kelly and Melissa. I have to tell you the truth about something."

His eyebrows rose. "Sounds serious."

She nodded.

"Then come on over here and sit." He gestured to a big leather chair in front of the fireplace, then settled into the one beside it.

Janet liked the arrangement. She didn't have to look directly into his eyes while she talked. She began slowly, telling him about the summer she had spent with Lone Wolf. Then she repeated all of the stories he had told her about their ancestors being forced out of Texas.

"I resolved then that I wanted to make it right. I came here wanting to get that land back. If I could have found a legal way to do it—which I couldn't, by the way—I would have taken White Pines from you," she summarized.

There, it was all out in the open. She glanced over at him to gauge his reaction. To her astonishment, he smiled.

"I know," he admitted without batting an eye. "I've known for some time now."

"You've known," she repeated blankly, then wondered why she was so surprised. Of course he would have put all the pieces together. He hadn't become a successful rancher without knowing how to read people. What she couldn't seem to absorb was the fact that he had taken the discovery so well. Where was the ranting and raving she'd anticipated with such dread?

"And you still wanted to marry me?" she asked, bemused.

"How could I blame you for thinking of Lone Wolf and wanting to make amends for what happened to his father?"

"Why didn't you say anything?"

He shrugged. "Because you needed to figure out you could trust me enough to tell me the truth."

Tears stung her eyes. "Oh, Harlan."

"Hey," he protested, "don't start crying. I won't say I wasn't mad as a wet hen when I first figured out what was going on after Jenny spilled the beans about where Lone Wolf had once lived. Then I did a little research of my own. I discovered you had cause to come here and do what you were doing. I'm sorry you couldn't figure out a legal way to do it."

"But you see, then, why we can't get married," she said. "I just wanted you to know that it's not because I don't love you. It's because you'll never know for certain if it's you I want or White Pines."

"Darlin', my ego's in no danger of being deflated by uncertainty," he said, waving off that argument dismissively. "You'd never marry a man you didn't love. There's never been a doubt in my mind about that."

She refused to accept that. It was too easy. She deserved his hatred or, at the very least, his disdain. Yet he was still claiming he wanted to marry her.

"I have to go," she said, leaping to her feet and heading for the door.

He stepped in front of her. "Not without saying yes to my proposal. All our cards are on the table now. There's no reason to say no."

"I can't," she insisted, guilt and confusion tumbling through her. How could she say yes, when she didn't deserve the love of a man like Harlan?

"Mom!" Jenny wailed from the doorway.

Her gaze shot to her daughter. "How long have you been standing there?"

"Long enough to know you've flipped out completely. I can't believe you'd do something like this." With that she whirled and ran from the room.

Janet stared after her in shock, then turned back to Harlan. "I have to go after her."

He nodded. "Go. But this isn't over, Janet. Not by a long shot."

Jenny refused to say a single word during the entire drive home. She huddled against the passenger door and stared out the window, her expression sullen. Janet felt as if they were right back where they'd been when they'd first arrived in Texas. All of the progress she and Jenny had made over recent weeks had disappeared in an instant back in Harlan's study.

When they got home, Jenny headed straight for her room.

"Jennifer, get back here."

"I'm not in the mood to talk."

"Then you'll listen," she said. But once Jenny had reluctantly sprawled in a chair in the living room, she had no idea what to say. She wasn't even entirely sure why her daughter was so furious. She could hazard a guess, though.

"Look, I know you like to think of Mr. Adams as the enemy," she began. "But he's not. And there's no need for you to concern yourself that I'll marry him, anyway, because I turned him down.''

Jenny shot her a look of disgust. ''Jeez, Mom, don't you think I know that? I heard everything.''

''Well, then, why are you acting as if I've gone over to the enemy?''

''You've got it all wrong. I think you're making the worst mistake of your life, if you don't marry him.''

Janet's mouth dropped open. ''What?''

''I know why you're turning him down, though. It's not because of all that stuff about Lone Wolf and the land.''

''Of course it is,'' Janet insisted.

''It is not. Not really. He told you that stuff didn't matter to him anyway. You're saying no because of your own stupid pride.''

The accusation stung, not because it was unjustified, but because somewhere deep inside it rang all too true. ''I don't have any idea what you're talking about,'' she said stiffly.

''Oh, puh-leeze!'' Jenny retorted. ''When you left Daddy, you swore you'd show him you could stand on your own two feet. You're afraid if he hears you're marrying some rich guy, he'll think you've sold out.''

Before Janet could gather her wits to react to that, Jenny went on.

''Do you think it even matters to him what we're doing?'' she said with adolescent bitterness. ''He never calls. He never comes to see us. The only time you hear anything at all is when he sends a child support check. I think you'd tear that up, if you could.''

It was true. Only the awareness that the money belonged to Jenny kept her from doing just that. Every cent was in an account in her daughter's name, meant for her college education.

"So what's your point?"

"Just that you're afraid if you marry anyone, much less a guy like Harlan Adams, Daddy will see it as an admission that you couldn't make it on your own. Like he really cares," she said with more of that angry sarcasm Janet had never heard before.

Feeling both bemused and under attack, she asked carefully, "Do you want me to marry Harlan?"

"I want you to be happy, Mom. It's all I ever wanted. And Harlan's a pretty cool guy. I knew that the minute he caught me after I stole his truck. He didn't freak out, like some guys would have. I've been pretty rotten sometimes since and he hasn't hated me for that, either."

She shrugged. "Maybe I was testing him, to see if he'd be like Daddy and abandon me just because I wasn't behaving suitably." The last was said in precisely her father's judgmental tone.

Janet sighed heavily. At last the reason behind Jenny's behavior for the past few months was coming clear. She'd lost her father, even when her behavior had been exemplary. She'd been testing, not just Harlan, but before that, Janet herself, to see if they would abandon her at the first sign of trouble. Now her gaze was fixed anxiously on Janet's face. "So, will you at least think about it?"

"I'll think about it," she promised.

She did little else for the next twenty-four hours. By morning, she thought she had figured out a way to prove to Harlan that it was him—and him alone—she loved.

Chapter Fifteen

When Harlan turned up to take Janet to lunch the next day, he sensed right away that something had changed. He couldn't tell exactly what it was, just a bit more color in her cheeks, maybe a glint of confidence in her eyes.

"I have some papers here for you to sign," she said when he walked through the door.

He frowned at her businesslike tone. Was she about to get into the land ownership issue, after all? Had she found some blasted loophole she hadn't admitted to the last time they'd talked?

"What sort of papers?" he asked suspiciously.

"It's a legal agreement."

His wariness doubled. "Who are you representing?''

''Myself.''

His heart slammed against his ribs. So it was about the land.

''Suing me, are you?'' he asked, keeping his voice light, when he wanted to lay into her at the top of his lungs for spoiling everything, for not trusting him to do what was right.

Her mouth curved into a sensuous smile that made his heart go still. If that smile had anything to do with a land deal, he'd eat his hat. But what, then?

''You'd love that, wouldn't you?'' she taunted. ''You're never one to back down from a good fight.''

''Gets the juices flowing, that's for sure.'' He reached for the papers and began to read. His eyes widened at the first line. ''A prenuptial agreement? What the hell is this for?''

''It's an agreement between you and me, before marriage, guaranteeing that I won't take a dime of your money if the marriage ever breaks up.''

''Like hell!'' he exploded, too furious to even think about the fact that she was apparently agreeing to marry him. He didn't like the terms she had in mind. He didn't like 'em one damned bit! ''I'm not going into a marriage thinking about how it's going to end. The day you and I get married it will be forever, Janet Runningbear, not one of those blasted things where one of us skedaddles at the first hint of trouble.''

To his astonishment, she chuckled. ''I had a feeling you were going to say something like that, so I made a few alterations from the traditional prenup agreement. Perhaps you should read the details.''

He was about to rip it to shreds when a phrase caught his eye. Something about guaranteeing that White Pines would remain with his sons.

''What's this?'' he asked.

''Just putting what's right in writing,'' she said. ''I want to be sure there's never a doubt in your mind about why I'm marrying you. Read the rest. See how it suits you.''

The next paragraph legalized his adoption of Jenny as his daughter. He couldn't have been more flabbergasted if they'd let him win at poker. He searched Janet's face for proof that this wasn't some sort of diabolical hoax.

''She's sure about this?'' he asked, not able to control the hint of wonder in his voice.

''She and I talked it over this morning. It's what she wants. She wants to be your daughter.'' Her gaze caught his. ''If you'll have her.''

Tears stung his eyes. ''It would make me proud to have her call me daddy. Your ex-husband, though, he won't mind?''

''He'll have to be consulted, of course, but I don't see why he would, especially if it would let him off the hook with the child support he sends so grudgingly.''

He couldn't believe that everything was finally coming together just the way he'd imagined. He cupped Janet's face in his hands. ''You're dead serious about this? You're not going to back out of this on me, are you?''

She shook her head. "Not a chance."

"You know we're going to be butting heads every now and then. That's just the way of marriage."

"So I've heard. Your daughters-in-law have informed me what it's like to be married to a stubborn Adams."

"Traitors," he muttered, but he was smiling. He knew he owed the three of them for making Janet take a second look at his proposal and forcing her to shed her conscience of that secret she'd been keeping. He had a feeling he might owe Jenny, too. She'd promised to intercede in his behalf and it looked as if she had.

He studied Janet intently, not quite able to believe that she was almost his. She was so beautiful she took his breath away. He'd be counting his blessings till the day he died.

"How soon?" he asked.

"How soon what?"

"When can we get married? You want a big to-do or can we sneak off and keep it from those brats of mine?"

"It doesn't have to be big, but I want those wonderful children and grandchildren of yours to be there. We're going to start this off as a family," she insisted. "No more secrets. Understood?"

"Don't look at me with those big brown eyes of yours," he accused. "I'm not the one who was hiding what I was up to. You knew from day one what I wanted from you."

She grinned and looped her arms around his neck. "And what was that?"

"This," he said, and settled his mouth over hers. He ran his tongue along the seam of her lips until they parted. The taste of her was sweet as peppermints and far, far more intoxicating.

"If you hadn't said yes soon," he declared when his breathing was finally even again, "I'd have had to kidnap you and haul you off to some justice of the peace."

"And what if I still hadn't been willing?"

"I'd have used all of my considerable influence to see that the ceremony came off anyway," he declared, liking the immediate flare of temper in her eyes.

"You can't expect to bully me into giving you your way, Harlan Adams."

"Who's talking about bullying?" he said, closing a hand gently over her breast and teasing the nipple until he could feel it harden even through the silk blouse and the lacy bra he knew was underneath. "There are other ways to tame a skittish filly."

His expression sobered then. "I love you, Janet Runningbear. I'll make you happy. For all my teasing and taunting, you can count on that as a solemn promise."

"I love you, too, Harlan." The smile she turned on him then was radiant. A bride's smile. "It ought to be downright fascinating, don't you think?"

"What?"

"Our marriage."

He grinned back at her. "I'm counting on it."

Janet stood at the back of the church barely a week later and fussed with her white antique lace dress. "Are you sure I look okay?" she asked Jenny for the thousandth time.

"You look beautiful, Mom. Every hair is in place," she added, anticipating Janet's next question. She twirled in her own dark rose dress. "How about me? Do I look grown-up?"

"Too grown-up," Janet declared, wondering where the time had flown.

It seemed only yesterday that her daughter had been small enough to rock to sleep in her arms. And yet she wouldn't go back for anything. Jenny was going to make her proud one day. She was bright, spirited and intrepid. With Harlan as a father, she could be anything she chose to be.

Lone Wolf would have been satisfied with how far his descendants had come and how far they would continue to go, she thought. Perhaps she had fulfilled her promise to him, after all.

"Isn't it time yet?" Jenny asked. "What's taking so long?"

"Blame me," Harlan said from the doorway to the church, taking them both by surprise.

"Harlan," Janet protested. "You shouldn't be back here. It's bad luck."

"You and I have one last detail to settle before you walk down the aisle," he said, pulling a thick packet of papers from his pocket and handing them to her.

Janet regarded him warily. "What's this?"

"It's one of those prenuptial things you seem to like so much. I ripped up yours," he said, handing her the shreds of paper as proof. "I set out a few terms of my own."

Janet allowed the remains of her prenuptial agreement to filter through her fingers, then took Harlan's papers with a hand that trembled. She wasn't sure what last-minute fears might have driven him to clarify the status of things between them in writing.

"Read it," Harlan insisted, putting an arm around Jenny's shoulders and giving her a squeeze as Janet began to scan the familiar legal language.

She'd read no more than a clause or two before her gaze shot up to meet his. "This isn't a prenuptial agreement at all. It's a will."

"I knew a fine lawyer like you would see that right off," he taunted.

"You're putting Jenny into your will as one of the heirs to White Pines?" she whispered, incredulous.

"She'll be my daughter," he said firmly. "She's entitled to her share, not just as my daughter, but as a descendant of Lone Wolf's."

Tears welled up in Janet's eyes. "The land should belong to your sons. They were raised on it."

"'Just putting what's right in writing'," he insisted, quoting her. "If things had gone differently a hundred years ago, maybe you'd have been raised on this land. Maybe Jenny would have been born here. I just see that paper as bringing things full circle.''

''She'll probably put a shopping mall on it,'' Janet threatened.

Harlan winced, but stood firm. ''That'll be her choice,'' he said, gazing fondly at Jenny, who was staring at the two of them in stunned silence. ''Thanks to you, she has a good head on her shoulders and good, decent values. She'll make us both proud.''

Oblivious to wedding day conventions, which had already been shot to blazes anyway, Janet threw her arms around his neck and kissed him. ''Oh, Harlan, I do love you.''

He grinned. ''It's a darn good thing, 'cause there's no way you'd get out of this church today without saying 'I do'. I can't wait to walk down that aisle in there, so the whole world will know how proud I am to be your husband.''

''Even if I don't change my name from Running-bear to Adams?''

He winced. ''Even then,'' he conceded. ''You've worked hard to be who you are. I guess you've earned the right to call yourself whatever you want, as long as it's me you come home to at night.''

''Count on it,'' she said softly, then took his hand. ''Since we've already made a mishmash of tradition, how about walking down that aisle with me to stand before the preacher?''

"Mom!" Jenny protested with a wail. "What about me?"

Janet grinned. "You can still go first. You'll probably have to revive the organist. She won't know what's going on."

"That's exactly why I'm so anxious to get started on this marriage," Harlan declared, winking at Jenny. "With your mom around, there's no telling what'll happen next. I expect there will be surprises in store for all of us."

The ceremony wasn't nearly as topsy-turvy as their arrival for it, Harlan reflected late that night while Janet was changing into some fancy negligee he was going to take pleasure in stripping right back off.

He let his mind wander over the days and weeks since she'd come into his life and counted each minute among his blessings. He was so engrossed in his memories, he never heard a thing as she apparently managed to sneak up behind him and circle her arms around him.

"I love you, Harlan Adams," she whispered.

At the sound of those sweet words, a tremendous sense of peace stole through him. They were going to be so damned good together. Family had always been the most important thing on earth to him. Now, after losing his beloved Mary and his son, Erik, both in terrible tragedies that had taken them too soon, his family circle was going to grow once more. His life was once again complete.

''I love you, Janet Runningbear. And I love the daughter you've brought into my life.''

Her eyes lit with a teasing glint. ''Who knows, Harlan? Maybe I'll give you another one before we're done.''

It was a good thing she slid into his lap and kissed him then, because he was too darned flabbergasted to say a single word. A father again? What an astonishing, incredible idea! One thing for sure, any child they had together was bound to be a hellion.

He could hardly wait.

Epilogue

By golly, if Janet didn't go and make good on her promise. Barely nine months to the day after their honeymoon, Harlan found himself pacing the hallways at the hospital waiting for her to give birth. The whole danged family was there, fussing and carrying on, teasing him unmercifully about getting a second chance at parenthood.

"Maybe this time you'll get it right," Cody teased.

"There's not a thing about the way I did it the first time that I'd do over," he shot right back, then sighed heavily. "Except with Erik. I'd do that over if I could."

Luke put his arm around him. "Daddy, Erik made his own choices."

Jessie stood on tiptoe to kiss his cheek. "That's right. It's time to let it go. Besides, this should be a happy occasion. We should be concentrating on the new baby, not sad memories."

Jenny, who'd been standing impatiently in the corridor outside the delivery room for the past hour, came up in front of him and scowled. "I just don't get it. What's taking so long? And why aren't you in there with her?"

"Because he'd be telling the doctor what to do, that's why," Cody chimed in. "The delivery room staff signed a petition to keep him out."

"But you took those classes with Mom and everything," Jenny protested. "Now she doesn't even have a coach in there with her. If I'd known you were going to chicken out, I'd have taken the classes."

Just then a nurse appeared in the doorway. She zeroed straight in on Harlan. "Mr. Adams, your wife is asking for you."

His breath caught in his throat. "The baby?"

"Should be here any minute now," the nurse said. "She says you'll probably only have to suffer through a contraction or two."

When his sons heard that, they hooted. "Now we know," Jordan taunted. "Janet was terrified you were going to faint in there, wasn't she?"

"We reached an agreement is all," Harlan said defensively.

The truth of it was, Janet had fought like a demon to keep him from seeing her in pain. He'd fought just as hard to be in that delivery room. He'd missed out on the birth of his sons, because that was the way of the world back then. He'd regretted it more than he could say. This time he wanted to be there for the miracle, just one of many to come into his life since the day he'd met Janet and Jenny.

As promised, he walked through the door of the delivery room just in the nick of time. Janet's face was bathed in sweat, but the smile she turned on him was enough to fill his heart to overflowing. He clasped her hand.

"I hear you're doing great," he said.

"So they tell me," she said, suddenly clenching his hand in a grip so fierce he thought for sure the bones would break. "This is it."

"Sure is," the doctor agreed. "That's it, Janet. Come on. Just a little more."

Harlan's incredulous gaze was fixed on the doctor, watching his concentration, then the smile that slowly spread across his face just as he lifted their brand-new baby into the air.

"It's a girl," he announced. "A big one, too. Pretty as her mama."

If there'd been a chair close by, Harlan would have collapsed onto it. Tears welled up in his eyes as he turned a tremulous smile on Janet. "A girl," he repeated softly. "Another daughter."

"I promised, didn't I?" Janet whispered.

He leaned down and pressed a kiss filled with gratitude and love to her lips. "Thank you for my two girls," he murmured. "Most of all, thank you for loving me and making my life complete."

Just then a nurse approached carrying their daughter in a pretty pink blanket. "Here she is, Mr. Adams. Would you like to hold her?"

An awe unlike anything he'd ever before experienced spread through him as he took that precious bundle into his arms and gazed down into his daughter's tiny, scrunched-up face.

"She is so beautiful," he said, barely getting the words past the lump in his throat. "What are we going to name her? Have you decided?"

"I had a thought, but I wasn't sure how you'd feel about it," Janet said.

"What?"

"I was thinking of naming her Mary Elizabeth," she said, watching his face intently.

He was stunned by the generous, unselfish gesture. "Wouldn't you mind naming her for Mary?"

Eyes shining, she reached for his hand. "It's something I'd like very much to do for you and your sons. I was thinking we might call her Lizzy."

He gazed down at the child in his arms and grinned. "Lizzy, huh? What do you think?"

Mary Elizabeth Adams opened her tiny mouth and wailed. There was no telling if that was a sign of approval or dissent, but Harlan took it as a positive reaction. He smiled at Janet. "Lizzy, it is."

"So," she said, as they wheeled her and the baby to her room, "do you think there are any more surprises in store for us?"

"You bet," he promised. "They're around every corner."

* * * * *

COMING NEXT MONTH

#1021 MOLLY DARLING—Laurie Paige
That's My Baby!
Rancher Sam Frazier needed a mommy for his little Lass—and a
wife in the bargain. He proposed a marriage of convenience to
Molly Clelland—but he never dreamed he'd long to call the instant
mother his Molly darling....

#1022 THE FALL OF SHANE MACKADE—Nora Roberts
The MacKade Brothers
Footloose and fancy-free, Shane MacKade had a reputation as a ladies'
man to uphold, and he took his job seriously. Who would have thought
a brainy beauty like Dr. Rebecca Knight would cause this irrepressible
bachelor to take the fall...?

#1023 EXPECTING: BABY—Jennifer Mikels
An urgent knock at the door introduced Rick Sloan to his neighbor—
Mara Vincetti, who was about to give birth. Next thing Rick Sloan
knew he was a father figure for the new single mom and her baby!

#1024 A BRIDE FOR LUKE—Trisha Alexander
Three Brides and a Baby
When sister-of-the-bride Clem Bennelli met brother-of-the-groom
Luke Taylor, it was a case of opposites attract. They agreed theirs
would be a passionate, no-strings-attached relationship—but neither
one expected to want much, much more....

#1025 THE FATHER OF HER CHILD—Joan Elliott Pickart
The Baby Bet
Honorary MacAllister family member Ted Sharpe was carefree and
single. But secretly he yearned to be a husband and a father. And
when the very pregnant divorcée Hannah Johnson moved in next
door—he lost his heart, but found his dreams.

#1026 A WILL AND A WEDDING—Judith Yates
Commitment and marriage were two words Amy Riordan never
believed would apply to her. After meeting similarly minded
Paul Hanley, however, she began to think otherwise—and now
the word "wedding" was definitely in her future!

STEP

INTO

THE

A collection of award-winning books
by award-winning authors!
From Harlequin and Silhouette.

Available this April

TOGETHER ALWAYS

by DALLAS SCHULZE

Voted Best American Romance—
Reviewer's Choice Award

Award-winning author Dallas Schulze brings you the romantic
tale of two people destined to be together. From the moment
he laid eyes on her, Trace Dushane knew he had but one
mission in life...to protect beautiful Lily. He promised to save
her from disaster, but could he save her from himself?

Dallas Schulze is "one of today's most exciting authors!"
—Barbara Bretton

Available this April wherever Harlequin books are sold.

It's time you joined...

THE BABY OF THE MONTH CLUB

Silhouette Desire proudly presents *Husband: Optional*, book four of RITA Award-winning author Marie Ferrarella's miniseries, THE BABY OF THE MONTH CLUB, coming your way in March 1996.

She wasn't fooling him. Jackson Cain knew the baby Mallory Flannigan had borne was his...no matter that she *claimed* a conveniently absentee lover was Joshua's true dad. And though Jackson had left her once to "find" his true feelings, nothing was going to keep him away from this ready-made family now....

Do You Take This Child? We certainly hope you do, because in April 1996 Silhouette Romance will feature this final book in Marie Ferrarella's wonderful miniseries, THE BABY OF THE MONTH CLUB, found only in— ▼ *Silhouette*®

™

Also available by popular author

SHERRYL WOODS

Silhouette Special Edition®

"I've been baby-sitting sweet little Lass,

but I'd never let on that I loved her rugged rancher daddy as much as I do her. Imagine my surprise when Sam Frazier proposed! Perhaps this is a marriage of convenience for now, but I can be a real mother to Lass—and maybe one day soon, my dream will come true and I'll hear my husband lovingly whisper my name...."

MOLLY DARLING
by
Laurie Paige
(SE #1021)

In April, Silhouette Special Edition brings you

THAT'S MY BABY!

Sometimes bringing up baby can bring surprises... and showers of love.

TMB496

Yo amo novelas con corazón!

Starting this March, Harlequin opens up to a whole new world of readers with two new romance lines in SPANISH!

Harlequin Deseo
- passionate, sensual and exciting stories

Harlequin Bianca
- romances that are fun, fresh and very contemporary

With four titles a month, each line will offer the same wonderfully romantic stories that you've come to love—now available in Spanish.

Look for them at selected retail outlets.

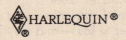

HARLEQUIN ®

Bestselling author

RACHEL LEE

takes her Conard County series to new heights with

A CONARD COUNTY *Reckoning*

This March, Rachel Lee brings readers a brand-new, longer-length, out-of-series title featuring the characters from her successful Conard County miniseries.

Janet Tate and Abel Pierce have both been betrayed and carry deep, bitter memories. Brought together by great passion, they must learn to trust again.

"Conard County is a wonderful place to visit! Rachel Lee has crafted warm, enchanting stories. These are wonderful books to curl up with and read. I highly recommend them."
—*New York Times* bestselling author
Heather Graham Pozzessere

Available in March, wherever Silhouette books are sold.

the exciting series by

Nora Roberts

Coming this April

THE FALL OF SHANE MACKADE
(Special Edition #1022)

Footloose and fancy-free, Shane MacKade had a reputation as a ladies' man to uphold. Who would have thought a brainy beauty like Dr. Rebecca Knight would cause this irrepressible bachelor to take the fall?

If you liked the first three books,
THE RETURN OF RAFE MACKADE (SIM #631),
THE PRIDE OF JARED MACKADE (SSE #1000), and
THE HEART OF DEVIN MACKADE (SIM #697)
you'll love Shane's story!

These sexy, trouble-loving men have been heading your way in alternating months from Silhouette Intimate Moments and Silhouette Special Edition. Watch out for them!

NR-MACK4